# THE INDIAN PARATHA
# &
# THE SYRIAN KIBBEH

*Love and destiny know no boundaries*

NOORUL AADHILA

**Chennai • Bangalore**

CLEVER FOX PUBLISHING
Chennai, India

Published by CLEVER FOX PUBLISHING 2023

ISBN: 978-93-56488-75-5



*First edition*

*"Edirne. The place that parted us is going to witness the union."*

**Noorul Aadhila**

# Dedication

*To my husband Akram, for the constant
support and motivation.*

# Author's Note

Dear Readers,

Having wanted to write a novel since my teens, I, Noorul Aadhila, have written my debut novel now. Currently based in France, I got an eyeful of desperate Syrian immigrants whose plight had a strong impact on me. Bringing in my writing zeal, I have put together a work of factual fiction by blending elements of reality and fiction. I have fleshed out the stories of Syrian immigrants, shedding insight into the harsh realities they face while also highlighting their resilience and strength in the face of adversity, and have created a gripping narrative that I hope will captivate you.

I'd like to take a moment to share with you some insights into my creative process, the inspiration behind this story and the historical context of real events that influenced its narrative.

*The Indian Paratha and The Syrian Kibbeh* began as a spark of curiosity ignited when I saw immigrants from Syria on the roads and at several traffic signals in France. They looked miserable and forlorn. Thus, backed by extensive research, I embarked on this journey, drawing characters from both historical accounts and the depths of my imagination who would carry the weight of the story. I want to emphasize that this is a work of fiction, and while inspired by real atrocities in the war zone of Syria, the Christchurch attacks in New Zealand, Angelina Jolie's speech on Syrian refugees in the UN, victim impact statements, and survivors' experiential stories.

In closing, I hope that this book resonates with you on both an emotional and intellectual level. It is my privilege to share this story with you, and thank you for joining me on this literary journey through the pages of *The Indian Paratha and The Syrian Kibbeh*.

# Disclaimer

This novel draws inspiration from various real incidents and factual information. Historical facts, research, and personal experiences have influenced the author. However, the story should be regarded as a work of fiction. While the backdrop and certain events may bear resemblance to actual occurrences, the characters in the novel are fictional. Any similarities to real individuals, living or deceased, are purely coincidental. The novel's plot is a product of the author's creative interpretation of historical events or situations. Details may have been altered, combined, or imagined to suit the narrative. While efforts have been made to portray certain aspects of the story accurately, it is not intended to be a documentary or a factual account. The author has taken creative liberties to enhance the storytelling and provide readers with an engaging and imaginative experience.

# Chapter 1

The colossal Pierre de Coubertin stadium was packed with spectators on all four sides, filling the expansive seating area. The fans created an aroma of enthusiasm by cheering for their team as both teams entered the stadium court and lined up in a row across from each other. Their excitement brought forth a unique, electrifying ambience to the stadium, and the pregame rituals that set the stage for the game began. Following the announcement of each player's name and jersey number, they waved to the crowd and acknowledged the applause. As a show of sportsmanship, both teams walked sequentially in opposite directions letting each player on one team to do a friendly high five with every player on the other team. Standing at the centre of the court, both teams, along with the referee, decided which team would start and on which side of the court. The players returned to their benches to discuss the game plan with their coaches.

Riya closed her ears tight with her hands as she entered the stadium. The noise the crowd made to cheer the players was immense and piercing. Riya and her friends began climbing the stairs to their seats in the second row from the top, but she could neither focus on the steps nor find their seats. She was fascinated by the view of such a huge stadium, the bright lights, and the players of two teams positioning themselves on the court. Then, the music band played a tune, she didn't know if it was their anthem or just a random tune. The beat and tempo were so enticing that she started vibing to the rhythm. She glanced at her friends, who were still searching for their seats.

"Is it from H10 or H11?" asked Sylvie, one of her friends.

"From H10 to H15," replied Layla, another friend.

She was blindly following the two of them, and she was followed by the other two, Valerie and Ai. In a few seconds, her friends finally found their seats and settled down.

"Riya, did you check out the rules of Handball?" Sylvie asked.

"Uhmm… Actually, I didn't have the time to…" Riya started making up an excuse.

"Okay, you were least interested in this Handball match, but only if you had read a little about the rules, you would be able to understand the game," blamed Sylvie.

Riya tried to defend herself, "Not this particular Handball match. I'm not interested in any match, sport or games. I find sports unappealing, and these are not my things. I have never watched a match in my life even on the television and I don't understand them too. We could have planned a trip to the Chateau de Fontainebleau. Oh my god, its architecture and artistic grandeur are simply breathtaking. I would much rather spend my time exploring…"

Valerie interrupted them, "C'mon girl, we're already here. Just watch what happens, and you'll get a grasp of it."

"At least tell me, when should I clap? Which is our local team? The ones in blue or white?" Riya asked

"Ah! Thank heavens you asked. Blue is Paris team, and White is Toulouse," answered Sylvie.

Riya took a glance at the court. On different sides of the court, both teams gathered in a circle. Perhaps to raise team spirit, she guessed.

"Ppphheww, not interested," she said to herself, taking her phone out of her pocket to check if she had received any message. She took a selfie with her friends and posted it on her Instagram page. Then, she scrolled for a few seconds, and when she was about to put it down, she just received a message.

```
Hey!

Hope the document is ready. And don't forget about the
presentation tomorrow.
```

"Ahh! Finally, I've got something to do with my phone. Thinking about work is way more beneficial than this match," she thought to herself opening her work mail app.

When she was just about to reply to the message, Sylvie grabbed the phone from her and slid it into her bag. She looked at Sylvie irritably, but Sylvie was fixated on the court. So, she had no other way out and decided to watch the match.

All the players swiftly moved to the other side of the court. Just as they reached there, one of them threw the ball into the net in a flash, which the goalkeeper missed to stop. And went the crowd at full blast.

"Shout, it's a goal" Valerie elbowed Riya.

Riya slowly started noticing each one of them on the court. They were fierce but were equally warm to their rivals. They ran back and forth from offence to defence after deftly passing the ball or scoring a goal. Some of them gestured to their teammates to coordinate movements. The only thing she understood was that if the players in blue jerseys strike a goal, it's time to shout and rejoice. She turned to look at the scoreboard. The Paris team had 4, and the Toulouse team had 3. She couldn't help but feel the intensity of the game as the score remained close. The crowd erupted with every goal, making her even more excited to see what would happen next.

"Are we winning?" She asked Valerie.

"It's just 4, and we have an hour more. Wait till the end. Because the climax is always very exciting," Valerie replied.

While Valerie explained, the Paris team scored another goal, making Riya yell and clap.

"Someone's finally into it!" said Sylvie, who didn't even bother to look at Riya.

"It is actually not that boring," Riya countered.

"FWEEEEEEEEEEEEET," blew the whistle of the referee.

"What happened? Why did they stop?" Riya asked inquisitively.

"It's a foul," replied Sylvie.

Riya's eagerness to grasp the game's complexities left no time for her friends to respond to the questions that began to flow one after the other.

"Why do they get another chance to throw the ball?"

"Why is that guy pushing him? Oh my! he is holding his T-shirt. Isn't this against the rules?"

"Why did he throw the ball to him?"

"It's not a goal, is it?"

After a list of questions, she noticed no one was replying to her. Hence, she sat quietly and started to observe the match and the players. Sylvie and Valerie exchanged amused glances, realising that Riya's initial disinterest had transformed into genuine curiosity and enthusiasm for the game.

Riya keenly watched each of the players in blue jerseys—their actions, attitude, hairstyle, and even their shoes. Simultaneously, she had an eye on the track of the ball, too. She found herself getting more and more engrossed in the game, trying to anticipate their next move. As the match progressed, Riya couldn't help but feel a growing sense of excitement and appreciation for the precision and skill displayed by the players as they effortlessly passed the ball to one another.

The Toulouse team passed the ball around before one of their players got it and leapt high to throw it into the net. For a moment, everybody thought that it was a goal. But the goalkeeper had blocked it. And everyone roared and chanted out his name,

"WA-SIM WA-SIM WA-SIM WA-SIM" exuding a high energy level and adding an emotional dimension to the match.

It took nearly ten minutes for Riya to realise that she had been staring at the goalkeeper, losing sight of the other players on the court, and ignoring everyone sitting around her. It was like only the two were in the entire stadium for those brief moments.

"FWEEEEEEEEEEEEET," the whistle went again, and the players retreated to their respective benches, reflecting on their performance.

"What happened? Is it a break?" Riya questioned.

"Yes" replied Sylvie.

"At the wrong time…" she muttered without being able to take her eyes off the goalkeeper, who was still on the court sitting down near the goalpost doing some stretches.

Ai peeped out from her seat and asked everyone to join her, "Come on, we'll go and fetch some snacks."

Sylvie and Valerie accompanied Ai as Layla was left to be with Riya. Layla got up and took a seat next to Riya.

"So, how do you enjoy the match?" asked Layla.

"I've just started loving it. Exactly from ten minutes before the break," said Riya and winked at her.

"Good that you find it interesting. Haven't you gone to any matches back in India?"

"No," her eyes were still fixed on the goalkeeper.

"Cricket is the most popular sport in your country, isn't it?"

"Yes, it is," and duh! The goalkeeper stood up and went to the side of the court, away from her sight. With the slightest disappointment and anger, she turned towards Layla with a long face.

"You still regret coming to this match?" Layla asked.

"No, no, no, I'm just tired" she replied and rested her head on Layla's shoulders still thinking about him.

Layla was talking about something that didn't reach Riya's ears. She shut her eyes and brought back the vision of him into her mind. She couldn't remember his hairstyle, neither his eyes nor his face, but something of him was lingering in her mind. And she wanted to see each of those closer.

"Uuff, too much crowd," said Ai, nearing the both.

"Ah, this girl here, she is already tired of watching a boring match," said Valerie and sat near Riya, extending a box of hot fries.

Riya took a fry from the box and savoured its warmth before continuing, "No, no, honestly…it was indeed getting interesting," she spilt out her expression. Fortunately, none noticed her excitement, and they were already into another conversation.

"Yesterday, I hit the Tuk Tuk Thai restaurant near Saint Augustin with some of my cousins," started Valerie.

"Ahh, I've been wanting to go there and try their Le tigre qui pleure," interrupted Ai.

"I've heard it somewhere. Where is it?" interrogated Layla

"In the 8ᵗʰ arrondissement. I tried it last week. C'était très Delicieux," said Sylvie and continued, "Valerie, did your cousin, Pierre, join you?"

"Yes, he did, and he asked many questions about Riya. I guess he likes you, Riya," said Valerie and turned towards Riya.

Everyone turned to look at Riya and realised she was not with them in the conversation. They noticed her lost in thought, yet the fries travelled from her hands to her mouth. Before they could ask her anything, the match began.

The band started playing the music again, the audience settled into their seats, and the players began moving to take up their positions. Riya's gaze wandered here and there throughout the stadium court, looking for that one person she was thinking about. She was fixated keenly on one side, completely ignorant that the players had switched sides. When she eventually tracked down the goalkeeper, her face filled with immense joy and a little shyness. She handed the box of fries to Layla and moved to the edge of the seat, getting ready to cheer up the team.

As the game started, Riya's excitement grew with each passing minute. She couldn't help but feel a surge of pride as she watched the goalkeeper make impressive saves. Though she didn't know when to shout, she managed to follow the other supporters of the team in the audience. She kept an eye on the fluctuating scoreline every now and then. After around twenty minutes of dodging, passing, and shooting the ball, the match was about to end, and everyone was waiting for that one goal. That one goal is to prevent the Toulouse team from defeating the Paris team. As tension in the atmosphere intensified, all the cheering and clapping subsided, and a hush fell over the crowd who were anticipating the last goal.

The players started the last round by throwing the ball at each other. Their intensity was palpable, and it seemed that each player had the determination to win and prove the relentless efforts that they had put into practice. The entire stadium's eyes were on the ball. The sound of the audience shouting for their teams was loud enough to compete against the live commentary and the band's music. Finally, the ball came to the last player and flew to the goalpost from his hands. And, it was Wassim who stood at the goalpost in the ready position, having his feet shoulder-width apart, slightly bending in the knees and back, hands set out in front, keenly observing the ball and reading the attacker's movement. While moving slightly to the left and right, he kept his gaze fixed on the ball. He hopped to the left, raising his left hand up in the air. In the twinkling of an eye, before you could know what happened, there was a loud cheer in the stadium. Wassim had successfully blocked the attacker's shot, sending the ball flying in a different direction.

"What happened? What happened?" fluttered Riya.

"It was a spectacular save," went the live commentary, and "Yay, we won!" erupted everyone around.

She didn't know how the goalkeeper blocked the ball in that close encounter but she knew he made his team win the match and elicited awe from the crowd. She locked her eyes on him as he dropped to the ground and prostrated for a few seconds. Within those few seconds, his other teammates flocked around him and hugged each other. Then, all of them went running to one side of the stadium where Riya could no longer look at him.

"Girls, shall we leave?" asked Sylvie and began walking towards the exit, and the other four followed her. As they made their way towards the exit, Riya couldn't help but feel a sense of disappointment. She had hoped to catch a glimpse of him one last time before leaving the stadium.

However, she understood it was time to go and reluctantly joined her friends in heading out of the stadium.

Once they reached the lower rows, Riya could see the players closer. Her eyes started searching for her hero again in the crowd. She was walking forward with her head tilted back. The moment she spotted him, he was looking at her already.

# Chapter 2

Riya was born in Kanchipuram, India, to a Tamil family. When she was ready to start school, her mother took her to Chennai, where her father worked as a financial analyst for a reputed global company. They visited their grandparents' home in Kanchipuram every month and spent quality time. She enjoyed visiting them for three main reasons. First, she was given unconditional love without any restrictions. Second, she cherished hearing her grandmother's tales, especially the folklore and debating the reasoning behind them. Third, she relished the food that her grandfather prepared for her.

When she was fifteen years old, her father was offered an international secondment to his company's Paris branch, which he gladly accepted. Her father left for Paris within a month and soon made all arrangements for Riya and her mother to join him there. Though Riya worried about going far away from her grandparents, she was persuaded that they would visit India every year.

However, Riya's parents were quite worried about how Riya would get along with this change. Much to their astonishment, Riya had an open attitude towards the new language, culture, conventions and lifestyle, embracing the change way too soon.

She established many local friends and observed how they talked, behaved, and did things to understand how they interacted and engaged in their daily lives.

In fact, she did these quicker than her parents. She started asking her mother for croissants and baguettes paired with Brie de Meaux or comté in the morning. Often, she prepares croque monsieur and quiche for dinner. During weekends, she nudges her mother to make a three-course meal exactly like the French. Though her parents were amazed, they enjoyed everything she did to immerse themselves in the culture.

She showed a mental willingness to accept and explore the new environment. She took the initiative and visited the nearby parks, museums, and other places of interest with her parents. She taught her parents what to look for in supermarkets. At times, she read French and explained it to them. She gathered recommendations and information from her friends and teachers about places for them to visit over the weekend. That is how she became aware of an entire stretch in the tenth arrondissement, between the famous train station Gare du Nord and La Chapelle. The area is known for its vibrant Indian community and streets with authentic Indian restaurants, grocery stores, and clothing boutiques, offering a taste of home for her. From eating parathas and dosas to buying colourful bangles and embellished clothes, she loves visiting the place when she misses India.

Every year, just as her parents had promised, they plan a trip to their home, back in India. She and her mother anticipate this time of the year, and once it's planned, they start making lists of things to buy from India, relatives to visit, places to go and much more. They stay in their hometown for one to two months, enjoying the native cuisine prepared by her grandmother and grandfather and meeting friends and relatives.

After her baccalaureate studies, she did her master's in Translation and Interpretation and is now working as a Conference Interpreter for the French government, thanks to her passion for languages. She always dreamed of working as an interpreter at the United Nations and is preparing for the CELP exams, too. She enjoys the challenges of interpreting for high-level meetings and diplomatic events. Riya believes she is driven by her goals and morals and has always seen herself as determined. The elegance and confidence that radiates from within is an added dash to her beauty.

* * *

Back in the stadium, when Riya's eyes locked with Wasim's for a brief moment, she felt a rush of excitement and connection. It felt as if their connection was unbreakable, even from a distance, and that he was going to enter her life for a reason. But before she could think of anything more, her friends pulled her forward from the crowd that pushed her from behind. So, she advanced, leaving her heart in the stadium with Wasim.

Riya had chanced upon many magical moments in life. The first time she got drenched in a waterfall. The first time she realised she was standing in front of one of the world's wonders- the Eiffel Tower. When she first sat on the banks of the River Seine. When she saw the beauty of Ladakh. When she visited the Lonar lake as it turned pink. When she explored Disney Land. When she visited the Bran castle in Romania and noticed that it was exactly as she had imagined in the fairy tales she had read. When she got the job that she liked. When she received her first pay packet. When she passed her driving test. But that evening in the stadium, it turned into the most magical moment in her entire life.

That night, hours before daybreak, she woke up checking the time on her phone. It was half past three. She tried sleeping again but couldn't. So, she got out of bed, covered herself with a blanket to comfort herself from the cold night breeze and went to the balcony in her room. It was silent out there, with a few cars passing occasionally. As quickly as she spotted raindrops on the road, she closed her eyes and inhaled deeply to draw in the petrichor emanating from the ground. There came an involuntary smile on her face. A bird sitting on the edge of a branch in a tree splayed its wings and shook vigorously in an effort to remove the raindrops from its feathers. The sound the bird made distracted Riya before she could totally appreciate the pleasure and open her eyes. Her attention turned upward towards the faded sky with all the light pollution, including streetlights, spotlights and building lights that curbed the beauty of the stars. Nevertheless, she could see the distant light from the Eiffel Tower's beacon every minute.

Every minute that the light passed her, the questions raced through her head, and the intensity increased.

"Why did he look at me?"

"Did he even look at me? Or perhaps someone else?"

"Was there someone behind me whom he saw?"

"No, the eyes, the eyes looked straight into mine."

"Has he seen me somewhere else before?"

"Did I happen to look familiar to him?"

She sighed and told herself, "Whatever it may be, he was cute," she hugged herself, burying her face in her hands shyly and went back to her bed.

She turned over in bed and tried to continue sleeping. But she couldn't sleep as her brain refused to quiet down and replayed the encounter in her mind over and over again. The memory of his gaze lingered, leaving her with a sense of curiosity and excitement. The anticipation of discovering the answers fueled her curiosity even more. She was baffled about meeting Wasim again and confronting him about the confusion caused. She thought about where she could search for him and how to initiate the conversation with him. Her initial assurance about whether he would remember looking at her, progressively gave way to uncertainty.

She wondered if he would even be willing to explain himself or if he would simply brush off the encounter as insignificant. Despite her doubts, she couldn't shake it off to find closure and put her restless thoughts to rest. She pondered the possible scenarios that could unfold during their meeting. As she tossed and turned, her mind raced with different approaches she could take to address the situation.

With this train of thoughts swirling inside her mind, she finally fell asleep. The next day, when she woke up, he was the first thought on her mind. So, she said to herself, "Okay. He's not gonna get out of my mind. I must start focusing on my exams. Now let me get going to the office."

* * *

Later that day, on her way home, she realised her legs were walking towards the stadium where she had seen Wasim the day before. She had no intention of going there. She didn't plan to meet him. But she did, however, wished to see him once again. She longed for him to be there at the moment, but at the same time, she was too nervous to face him.

Eventually, she reached the stadium and entered with utmost hesitation. She could hear the sound of the ball being thrown back and forth and the roars of players inside. While trying to recognize if Wasim was inside by paying close attention to their sounds, hoping someone might call out Wasim's name, she heard someone calling her from behind. She turned in fear and saw someone wearing the same blue jersey and a grinning smile.

"Are you searching for someone?" he asked.

"Uuhhmm..I..yeah…actually…yesterday" jabbered Riya. He interrupted with a dubious look.

"Wa… Wasim," finally she grabbed courage and stammered his name.

"Wasim? Come inside. He's in practice," he welcomed her inside.

She followed him, partly hiding herself behind him. Her eyes swiftly searched Wasim among the players on the court. She concentrated her search towards the goalpost where she had last seen him as the goalkeeper. But all of a sudden, someone sitting on the side of the court stood up and came running towards her. And yes, it's the man of her dreams.

She stood still without knowing what to do, what to say and how to react to him. She could feel her face becoming hot, her palms becoming wet, and her legs getting frail in anxiety. She firmly grounded her legs to the ground and held her mobile phone tightly in her hand. She couldn't see anything around her as her eyes became blurry. She blinked her eyes as fast as possible to see clearly before Wasim reached her. Wasim stood before her, panting and looking deep into her eyes. She couldn't take that strong gaze and lowered her head down.

"Any news?" asked Wasim, waiting eagerly for a favourable answer.

Riya was clueless. "News?" she echoed.

"I saw you yesterday after the match. But before I recognize you, you left. I was thinking about you all night. I mean… I believed you had something to tell me and was worried about how I would find you again." replied Wasim.

Riya now understood that he had mistook her for someone else. Though this eased her a little, it also disheartened her. She closed her fists tight as if she wanted to hold on to something that was getting out of her grasp. Because somewhere in her heart, she slightly believed that he fell in love with her at first sight, which was why he locked eyes with her. Though her brain realised that it was very silly and dumb of her to think that way, her face was trying to expose the sharp pain stabbing from within. She furrowed her eyebrows, gulped down her pain and began to clarify, "Uhhmmm…You mistook me for someone else. I…I saw you yesterday during the match and you too saw me as if you knew me. I got confused and…"

Before she could complete it, Wasim interrupted, "I'm terribly sorry, I confused you with someone very important," and he turned back towards the court.

Riya watched him drift away aimlessly, exactly the opposite of how he had come running when he saw her. Things got cleared for her that he had no interest in her. Though she neither planned nor prepared for this meeting, she hoped she could talk with him for a while. Her eyes welled up as he walked away without even questioning why she was there despite the pathetic excuse that she had concocted. She fluttered her eyes repeatedly to push the tears back into her eyes. She muttered to herself, "Don't cry, don't cry, don't cry," and decided to leave before she started crying.

"I'm sorry again. By the way, did you come all the way here just to know why I looked at you?" Wasim came walking towards her again, but this time with a charming smile.

# Chapter 3

$A$s things got cleared now, Riya intended to reply with courage. She let her shoulders relax, kept her chin up, conceived that she was equally tall as Wasim, and looked straight into his eyes, "I saw you play yesterday, and I liked it so much. I couldn't stop thinking of it. And as you saw me till I was out of your sight, I…I…" she stopped for a while thinking how to complete.

Wasim quickly grasped what she was about to say and began to intrude, whilst a ball came flying approaching them. He swiftly caught it and ensured Riya was okay by looking at her eyes. Meanwhile, Riya, who didn't make out what just happened, was delving into each part of Wasim's face.

After asserting that she was all right, Wasim threw the ball back to the court, gestured to his friends and turned towards Riya again to show her the way out, saying, "Let's go out and talk."

"Actually, someone very important to me went missing a few years back. I didn't know what to do or where to search. That was when I met a girl volunteering in an NGO who offered to help me.

She said she could be able to find the person. But regrettably, I lost contact with her. When I saw you yesterday among the crowd, I mistook you for her as it's been so long since we met," clarified Wasim.

"I don't understand. Why didn't you get the help of the police? And are you waiting for a random girl to find the person you've lost for years?" questioned Riya.

"The story is complicated, and so is my life." shrugged Wasim, appearing not to share anything more about him.

By this time, they had reached the exit gate. Riya again understood that he had no interest in her and decided to leave. She wanted to indicate to him that she was in no way fascinated by him anymore. So, she shifted her gaze from Wasim to her phone as if preoccupied.

"All right, Wasim, nice meeting you. Take care, Bonne journée."

"How do you know my name?"

"I was among those who screamed your name after the last goal."

She smiled. He smiled back.

* * *

Riya returned home and went straight to her bathroom to shower. Standing under the warm water, she couldn't help but question her own emotions. She wanted to cry but couldn't. She couldn't understand what emotional state she was in. She was not sure if she had fallen in love with Wasim. If she was, how could she love someone she doesn't know even a bit? He could be a mere fascination, but why was she feeling numb after he showed his disinterest towards her?

She came out of the shower and got into her comfy loungewear. She asked her mother for a cup of coffee and sat at the coffee table on the balcony near the kitchen. After the tough winter loosened its hold, the faint breeze of Spring's air coursed past her face. The loose strands of her hair waving down on both sides of her face flew and billowed. She closed her eyes to take pleasure in it. As her hair flew liberally without any constraints, so changed her mind. She stopped thinking about Wasim, hoping the pause of thoughts would help her get over him. Instead, she focused on the fresh aroma of coffee and the gentle rustling of leaves in the nearby trees.

Her mother came with two cups of coffee and sat with her. "What's the matter?" she asked Riya.

Riya, who just decided not to think of Wasim, chose not to talk about him either.

"Let it go, Mom. What's for dinner?" inquired Riya. "I'm making chapatis with chickpea curry."

"Why chapatis? Can we have paratha today?"

"I've already kneaded the dough for chapatis. Okay, I'll make just two for you. By the way, look here: two million views for my Tom Yam soup video."

"Wow, Mom. You are doing great. What are you going to make in your next video?"

"Haven't decided yet. Either Tiramisu or Blueberry cheesecake."

"Blueberry cheesecake. I feel like eating cheesecake."

"Okay, decided then. Baby, shall I ask you something?"

"Yes, Mom."

"A boy was standing near a coconut tree. Two of his friends, standing far away, gestured to him to come to them. Why?"

That brought a genuine smile to Riya's lips involuntarily. Because her mother always asks questions like these and gives funny answers. Though they are the least funny, Riya and her dad enjoy her mother's jokes.

"Because they feared a coconut might fall on his head?" Riya tried answering.

"No. They are standing far away. They couldn't be heard if they shouted. That is why they gestured to him," explained her mother.

They both burst out laughing. And after continuing the conversation with her mother for some time, Riya brightened up and felt good. But how could she completely forget Wasim? His thoughts were waving in and out of her mind.

* * *

Three days later, on Friday mid-day, people were flocking inside the mosque, among whom Wasim entered the courtyard of the mosque. He stood in the centre, watching men and women of various ages dressed in clean, bright clothes and children running into the front hall. He closed his eyes briefly and took a deep breath as he slowly inhaled the pleasant perfumes of the people around him. He slowly opened his eyes, listening to the lively talks and merry waves of laughter surrounding him. He finds solace in this aura when he attends the congregational prayer every Friday in the mosque.

Once the imam started the sermon, everyone gathered inside the prayer hall and started worshipping. All of a sudden, they heard three consecutive gunshots. The imam stopped the recitation for an instant and continued again.

As he began again, they heard multiple gunshots outside, and a man shouted, "Someone is shooting our Muslim brothers and sisters." Before anyone inside could realise what was happening, they saw a man with a rifle wearing all black, with a military-style helmet over his head and covering his face with a mask. A pandemonium erupted.

Wasim stood there motionless, seeing the gunman walk across the door. Gunshots were coming continuously through the window, and the man standing next to him in prayer dropped down, bleeding from his shoulder and arms. Many ran towards the back exit, and some lay down on the floor, defending themselves. Wasim saw women and children crying and some getting shot. He was torn between running for their help and saving his life.

He covered his ears with both hands and bowed his head down as he started running to a pillar in the corner to hide behind it. At that moment, he heard many more sounds of gunshots, helicopters, tankers, rockets, and air strikes inside his head, bringing back some of his horrifying memories. The chaos triggered vivid flashbacks of the destruction that he had witnessed before. The deafening sound seemed to merge with haunting images of crumbling buildings and desperate faces, intensifying his inner turmoil.

When he reached the pillar and took his hands from his ears, he heard only a few gunshot sounds and a man hiding there talking over the phone in a hushed voice. He was convincing his mother that he was going to die and wanted to talk to her one last time. His mother on the other side of the call, who was able to hear gunshots, screamed in terror. People from a small room in the opposite corner of the hall called Wasim and the other man into that room to be safe. Wasim blocked the man from moving so as not to get shot. But the man thought he could be safe and started running towards the room, as fast as the bullet that came straight to his neck and fell down dead just a few feet away from the room.

Wasim's heart skipped many beats. He stopped breathing for a moment and found it difficult to swallow what he had seen just now. His eyes widened, and his eyebrows raised. He turned to the other side of the pillar, where he saw a boy who could be ten years old running towards him with dread-filled eyes. Wasim noticed that the boy's white shirt was stained with blood, and when he came closer, Wasim embraced the boy quickly into his arms and hugged him so tight that the poor little one could neither see nor hear anything.

After about two to three minutes of continuous gunshots, Wasim ordered the boy to stay right there, and he rushed out of the place where he was hiding, enraged, and decided to confront the gunman. He ran towards one of the doors in the hall, crossing several bodies lying on the floor. On the way, he picked up the gun the gunman appeared to have dropped and pulled its trigger. But there was no ammunition, as it was a shotgun with only three or four rounds. He still had it in his hand and ran outside, where he saw the gunman approaching his parked car, blocking the driveway.

After the initial shooting spree, the gunman was about to pull another weapon from his car to continue the attack. Wasim noted that the gunman was unarmed momentarily, and he hurled a heavy ceramic flower pot at him. But the gunman managed to dodge out.

Wasim shouted, "Who the hell are you?" The alarmed gunman swiftly grabbed an automatic rifle from the back seat of his car and started shooting at Wasim. Fortunately, Wasim took cover behind the other parked cars. Some people from inside the mosque shouted at him to return to the hall. Wasim refused and asked them to get in. When the gunman turned his attention to the hall again, Wasim bounced to his side and flung the shotgun he still had in his hand at him like a spear. The gun hit the gunman's car's windshield and shattered it.

The gunman was obviously frightened, as he probably thought that someone was shooting at his car. He knew he had explosives in his car and was worried that if the gunfire would burst his car, he'd not be able to escape. So, he hastily got in and drove off. But before exiting the mosque gate, he shot continuously at where he saw Wasim taking shelter without stopping his car. Despite Wasim weaving between cars to avoid the rallies of bullets, one of them hit him on his left hand near his chest.

Wasim tried running after him, holding the bleeding hand with his other hand. But before the gunman could disappear in the distance, Wasim saw three police cars surrounding the gunman's car. Two of those policemen approached the gunman's door, aiming their pistols at him before they dragged him down and handcuffed him.

* * *

Meanwhile, Riya, who was on a day off, was watching the news on television. She saw that the grand mosque of Pantin had been attacked and noticed Wasim was being taken on a stretcher behind the news reporter at the site where the breaking news had just happened. She was taken aback and, at once, hurried to the site without any thought.

Once she reached there, she noticed that the area was heavily cordoned off, and several people were standing along the way in groups, including reporters, cameramen, ambulances, a few police cars and lots of police. She couldn't digest that she was standing at a crime scene where dozens of people were killed. Her legs shuddered, and her hands turned cold. But her passion and fondness towards Wasim gave her an insane strength.

She walked towards a group of people and asked them, "Where have they taken the wounded?"

A woman in the group started sobbing, hugging her two small children.

Another man who was standing next to the woman came forward to take Riya aside and said, "I'm sorry, her husband's name is not on the injured list. They suspect he might have died. We don't know yet. She is not in a sensible state now." He took a deep breath and continued, "You can check the name of the person you are searching for in the injured list to confirm if…"

"No," Riya stopped him in a hushing voice. "I saw him alive, being taken in a stretcher… I mean on the television."

"Then, he must have been taken to the hospital or clinic nearby. You can check with that man standing near the ambulance. He is the official responsible for assisting people who come searching for the victims," he said, pointing a man a little farther.

Riya thanked him and hurried. She enquired the official about Wassim, who then requested more details from her. Poor Riya, who didn't know anything about Wassim except his name, not even his family name, was in a panic. The official informed her that four people were inside, all named Wassim, and advised her to wait until the names of the other three Wassims were ticked off. She waited more than two hours to be informed that they had received information on all four, but no Wassim was a young man in his twenties and a handball player. He also advised her to check the deceased list with another official.

That struck hard at Riya, and she was shattered. It was like a blast wave crashing down on her and rippling throughout her body. Her legs stood motionless, refusing to take the next step. She closed her eyes and brought Wassim's face to her mind. Along with that, she had an intuition that nothing of that sort could have happened to him. So, she nerved herself and went to check his name in the deceased list.

Along her way, till she reached the next person, she murmured to herself, "Wasim's name shouldn't be on the list, Wasim's name shouldn't be on the list, shouldn't be on the list, shouldn't be on the list, no, no, no." After checking the list, she rejoiced inside as she didn't find his name there. Looking at her relieved face, the official notified her that the details of many victims were missing and they were still in the process of gathering data. So, he suggested checking in the four hospitals around the area where the wounded had been sent to if Wasim had been admitted to any of those. Riya pinned her hope on his proposal and tussled over before she could confirm that Wasim had been admitted to the third hospital she tried.

28

# Chapter 4

"I couldn't believe something this grave could happen to you", Riya regretted.

"One of them had become a father only five days before. He only had the chance to hold his daughter once, and he was praying for her health when he was killed. He has not yet decided on the name of his daughter. His wife's parents, who came to take care of her, are killed too. The young woman, with her barely a week-old newborn, came running searching for her husband and parents, just to be informed that she had been left all alone in this ruthless world. Is this more grave than that?" Wasim started sobbing quietly.

Riya was shocked beyond words. She was able to see the emotional turmoil behind the blood and chaos she witnessed at the site. She stood next to him and put her hands on his shoulder. At once, he grabbed her and hugged her with all his might. Riya could feel the weight of Wasim's pain and desperation as he clung to her. With a throbbing heart, she rubbed Wassim's back as her tears were wetting his hospital clothes. Wasim suddenly loosened his clutch.

He looked at Riya with his bloodshot eyes and started speaking rabidly, "A woman…who came to check on her husband after hearing the gunshots, saw the gunman aiming towards her husband, ran before him, got shot and fell dead in her husband's hands."

Wasim couldn't stop. He wiped his face and continued, "What answer would a man give his wife… holding his probably 13-year-old dead son in front of her? The father… the father's face was awful, not knowing what to do with his son's body. They must have been thinking about all their unrealised dreams with their son." At this point, Wasim groaned loudly.

"Calm down. You better take rest now," Riya calmed Wasim, holding his hand tight and helping him lie down. Once he settled down to sleep, Riya slowly retrieved her hand and prepared to leave before he woke up. As she reached the door, a hospital attendant approached, inquiring if she was Wasim's friend. The attendant informed Riya that Wasim had said he had nobody to accompany him during his hospital stay.

Riya asked the attendant if they needed someone to look after Wassim. The attendant assured her that the hospital staff would take exceptional care of all their patients. However, more than that, Wassim required emotional support as he had been through an enormous trauma. So, Riya decided to stay with him at least until night. She confirmed with the attendant if he had received painkillers and sought information about what medicines were to be given once he woke up.

Riya called her mother to tell her where she was. Her mother was startled and bothered after knowing that her daughter had been to the crime spot that the whole world was talking about.

"Are you in your senses?" she yelled.

"Mom, Chill down. I'm not there anymore. I am in the hospital now, helping one of my friends. Poor him. He has none to take care of him."

"What? He has no one?"

"I mean…not in this city. His family must be somewhere else, I guess."

"You guess? Riya, this is…"

"Mom, Mom, Mom, I don't know him much. We barely met, but he has survived a trauma. He has been shot. Can you imagine? I saw a lot of blood–a lot–everywhere in the beautiful mosque. I didn't go inside, but outside the mosque, on the walls, on the parked cars, in the street, and on the clothes of people who were still standing there. My god, Mom! Ok... huff…. He needs my help in this difficult time. Please let me be here. Inform Dad, too. He'd certainly comprehend the situation."

"Riya, I see you becoming stronger, more than how we want you to be. I am in awe of your courage and kindness. Go ahead, darling. You know what to do and what's right. But be extremely safe because you are very precious to us."

"I love you, Mom."

"I love you too, baby."

She turned to Wasim, who was still asleep and sat on the chair beside his bed. Nothing was on her thoughts when she stared at his face at that precise moment, not even the terrible attack. A few days ago, she wished to look at his face closer. Now that she could admire him even more closely, she looked at his chaotic hair and drawn face. She reached to gently stroke his forehead but held back as she thought it was improper to touch someone without one's consent.

She asked herself, "Why do I like him so much? I know nothing about him, but here I'm to help. What if he asks me why am I here? What if I get into any trouble? Why do I feel I'm ready to face anything for him? What connection do we have? Is this what they call a past-life connection? I remember Grandma telling me about it. It's believed that we have seven lifetimes. When our bodies change for each lifetime, our eyes stay the same so one can recognise someone from a past lifetime. Maybe we were connected in our previous birth. I could recognise his eyes as if we had met and lived a life together. Of course, I don't find any logic in this, yet I prefer to give it the benefit of the doubt." She sighed heavily and rested her head on Wasim's bed, trying to take a quick nap.

* * *

Hours later, when Wasim woke up, he saw Riya looking through the window and talking to someone over the phone. Wasim wondered why she was still there and faked a cough, intending to call her. That is when he remembered that he hadn't asked for her name in their last meeting. Riya disconnected the call and walked towards him.

"Do you feel better now?" Riya came in front of Wasim.

"How can I? I see the tragedy again and again when I open my eyes, when I close my eyes, in my dreams, in my thoughts… God, it's terrible. Another blow yet again."

"Again?"

"Yes, my life has been a disaster."

"If I may ask, you don't look like French. Where are you from?"

"The land of curse," he paused, and after looking at Riya's confused face, he completed, "Syria."

There was a moment of stillness and gobs of appalling visuals called to Riya's mind. But she still managed to ask her next question to him, "When did you come to Paris?"

Meanwhile, Riya saw Wasim trying to sit up straight before answering her question. As he had difficulty moving his hand, he touched the dressed wound. He felt the burning heat inside, under many layers of covering. He cringed and gasped. She ran across to help him.

"You have been injected with painkillers earlier. Do you need more? The attendant has given a few tablets in case you need them," said Riya "Yes, please," replied Wasim in a painful tone.

Wasim looked at Riya fondly as she handed him a glass of water, followed by the tablets. He noticed how caring and concerned she was with him. Even a small act or word of consolation is substantial when someone is in pain. And here is this girl, caring for someone she barely knows. Her compassion and kind-heartedness manifested her inner beauty. That was the moment when Wasim started taking Riya seriously. He evoked the images of how passionately she looked at him the first time in the stadium, how she came all the way to the stadium just to see him again, and how she came to the hospital searching for him even after being conscious of how tragic the attack was.

He took the tablets from her and asked hesitantly, "I'm sorry, I know it's too late. But…, what's your name?"

"It's very, very late," reacted Riya with a childish frown on her face.

"We haven't met in such a situation where we first get introduced with our names," said Wasim, scratching his eyebrow in embarrassment.

"Ok. Here's your punishment. You have to guess it. It's a four-lettered beautiful name," smiled Riya.

Wasim chuckled and started guessing. "Aiza?"

"No."

"Sara?"

"No."

"Heba?"

"No. Okay, first, let me tell you that I'm from India. Do you know any Indian names?"

"I know just one."

"And what is that lucky name?"

"Riya," said Wasim, smiling mischievously.

"How is that even possible?" exclaimed Riya, widening her eyes.

Wasim swallowed the tablets and drank some water, making Riya wait anxiously.

Then he continued, "I heard you speaking to someone over the phone while I was sleeping."

He also mimicked her, "This is Riya. This is Riya. Can you hear me?" and laughed softly.

Wasim secretly appreciated how he had smiled and laughed in the past few minutes of his life after a long time. Riya smiled back and carried on.

"When did you come to France from Syria?" "After I reached Italy."

"Oh nice, you were in Italy! How did you come to Italy from Syria?"

"Through the Adriatic Sea. Croatia. Serbia. Bulgaria. Turkey. Aleppo, Syria. An arduous journey," uttered Wasim, fixating his eyes on the floor.

Neither he nor Riya looked at each other. Wasim was deep into those miserable thoughts, and Riya had no courage to face him at that instant.

# Chapter 5

"Life in Syria must have been miserable," Riya broke the silence. "Absolutely not," quavered Wasim, looking at Riya with his eyes welled up, and he went a little back in time,

*Life in Syria was beautiful. Yes, there were riots, protests, soldiers, tanks, and sometimes firings and bombings around us. In those few years, every morning, I woke up to see the skyline thick with smoke. Every night, I heard weird noises and woke up aghast. And in due course, I got used to them. Every now and then, we get word that buildings were bombarded, and many were killed and injured. I saw big war vehicles and army men with weapons from time to time. But in any case, I had my mother, father, and my younger brother, Aqeel, and I was happy inside our home. I had a place to call home; there was a roof above it protecting us from sun and rain, there was electricity and water, I had beds and blankets to sleep comfortably, I had home-cooked food, I had neat and clean clothes, I had friends and relatives, I was at ease.*

*But one night after dinner, while we were still sitting at the table, talking, my father received a phone call informing us that our factory had been bombed. My mother covered her mouth with both hands in dismay and was stock-still for some time. My brother and I looked*

*at each other, not knowing what to do or how to react, unable to comprehend the magnitude of what had just happened.*

*My father wanted to run to the factory right then, but my mother dissuaded him, saying he had to be safe, at least for us. He collapsed down on the floor, sitting with his hands on his forehead. I've never seen my father so desperate. My mother sat opposite to him and tried solacing, saying we still have our lives, and that is enough to rebuild whatever we have lost. Aqeel and I joined them, and we were all sitting together in that same spot for hours with heaviness in our hearts and chaos in our minds.*

*My father was constantly staring through the window. Maybe he was thinking about what to do with our factory and wondering what he would do next. We then received a phone call from my paternal uncle, who lives a few miles away. In a fearful tone, he apprised us that their apartment had been shelled, and there were fights on the street between civilians and soldiers. He also said that my cousin, who was ten years old then, had been heavily injured, and they were not able to reach the hospital. So, they did first aid at home and were getting ready to leave the country that night. He said he had some acquaintances in Europe and would contact them once they reached a safe place.*

*Now that the horror inched closer to us, we were paralysed, not knowing what to do. We spent some more time sitting closer to each other, listening to the sounds of explosions, helicopters, and commotion on and off all through the night. The sounds of destruction outside was a constant reminder of the danger that lurked just beyond our doorstep, making it impossible to sleep. I dumbly thought that that would be the scariest night ever in my life, unaware that I would see more scary nights ahead of me.*

*Imagine the plight of a sixteen-year-old boy in such a situation. Aqeel, he was just eight years old at that time. He was not even in the state to understand what was happening around us. He quietly listened to us talk and slept inside our mother's arms, certain that he was safe around us. Little did he know that the horrors of that night would shape his future in unimaginable ways.*

*My mother initiated the decision, "Let's speed away tomorrow at first light if we manage to remain alive tonight. Let's go somewhere," she said.*

*My father asked her in surprise, "Is this really you? You usually say you never want to leave the country!"*

*"Yes, if it's only for you and me, I would choose to live here or die here. But look at them. Look at the dreams that we have built inside them. Don't they have the right to live?" she sobbed.*

*"This is a hasty decision. Let's ponder over and…" my father started to explain when my mother cut off, "And? And what? And see our children die before my very eyes?" she raised her voice piercing the till-now silent conversation. My father went rigid, and his eyes stagnated at one random place, unable to take in this decision.*

*After a few minutes, I saw my father putting our passports and some money together in his locker, hinting to my mother that he had agreed to the decision. Seeing him, my mother hastened to pack a few clothes, some food to sustain ourselves for a few days, and other essential stuff.*

*My mother asked me if I wanted to take anything with us. What would I say? Yes, I want my favourite football, my cycle in which Aqeel and I go to school, my photography portfolio, my first plant that I grew in my garden, my new shoes that my father bought me on my birthday, or my comfiest fur blanket. Which of these could I take with me as a refugee? Nothing.*

*While my father was still grieving about the situation, my mother looked strong and determined. She started preparing me, saying I would have to take care of Aqeel if we had to lose them. She also talked about how I should continue my education, come what may, and how I should never let my essence and values fade away, that it's OK to be alone than to be in bad company, that it's OK to make mistakes and straighten them out once realised, that it's very important to respect others' feelings in every action done. And she was in a hurry to hand down to me everything possible, as she was too overwrought about our lives alone in this world. At that moment in time, I realised how, even in her worst imagination, we were safe, and she was ready to offer her life instead.*

*Hours later, as I was lying down in my father's lap, we received a call again. This time, it was from my maternal uncle who informed us about the demise of his wife and elder daughter after a grave air strike at his place hours before. Seconds later, after that call, we heard something flying above us. Before we realised what was happening, we were next. A huge flame struck, followed by the deafening sound of an explosion, and everything collapsed. I couldn't explain exactly what happened because I shut my eyes tight, and before I could feel anything, our home was crumbled to mere bricks, and we were amongst the ruins. For the next few minutes, neither could we see each other through the smoke and fume nor could we hear our cries.*

*My left leg got trapped under a big pile of bricks, and when I tried to bring it out, the pain intensified. I screamed out for my dad to help me, though I was not certain if he was alive. He reached out to me, dragging his body, bleeding and bearing the pain of many wounds. Once he helped my leg out, I hugged him back so tight and didn't want him to move away from me. He hugged me back and checked if I had any injuries, which fortunately I didn't, except a stabbing pain in the leg.*

*The acrid smell of smoke caused irritation in my nose, making it difficult to breathe. Yet I slowly stood up on my legs, and along with my father, we searched for Mom and Aqeel. As it was dark and hazy everywhere, we were unnerved to take our next step on the cracked floor, fearing that we would step on Mom and Aqeel or cause the rubble to fall down deeper. Slowly, my father managed to take a few steps farther, crying out for their names. He asked me to follow him step-by-step and not shout out loud, fearing that the militants would come inside knowing that somebody was alive and kill us to death. As we slowly progressed, I heard a heavy breathing sound near me, and it was my mother. She still held Aqeel securely in her hands. My father helped them come out of the rubble. Seeing Aqeel fully covered in black dust and my mother bleeding from her head was gut-wrenching.*

*Now that our entire home had been wrecked, we couldn't find my dad's locker, where he had kept our passports and money. However, he had some extra money and the car key in his pant pocket. So, we came out by stepping over the debris, which was once our beautifully designed home with curated furniture and other household items we had collected in dribs and drabs. I left my heart there in our ruined, roofless house. At least we decided to move, there are still Syrians there living in that debris, in their roofless houses without water and electricity not being able to escape.*

*We didn't want to leave our home or our country. But, we were pushed to flee the place where we were born, grew up, made friends, made family, and built our livelihood. Until that night, I hoped to continue living in Syria with my friends and family in our beautiful home. But God had other painful plans for us.*

*We got into the car hastily before anyone could see us, and after a few minutes of driving, my father stopped near an ATM to withdraw more money. And that's when we noticed that Aqeel didn't speak a word since the strike, nor did he emote. While our faces were painful and enraged, his face was blank and expressionless. He didn't respond to our calls and cries but stared straight ahead. I, at once took him in my hands, wiped the grime off his face and shook him strenuously, crying out his name. Everything was in vain. My father suggested we take him to a doctor once we reach Turkey. So, I made him lay on my chest, and we started the journey.*

# Chapter 6

*A perilous journey it was. We didn't have a solid plan yet, but the prelude of that journey was to cross Syria's border safely. Since we were in the northern part of the country, Turkey seemed to be easily accessible for us. And we decided to make our choice of a safe place after reaching Turkey. On the way, my father told my mom that Turkey was actually to be a safe country for asylum seekers. They both were planning on getting the protection status and later a work permit, which would avail us of basic public services, including healthcare and education. He also contacted one of his acquaintances, who was ready to help us settle down once we reached Ankara. Furthermore, they intended to settle down there temporarily and return to Syria as soon as peace was restored.*

*The wakefulness of the previous night drifted me off for a really long time. I woke up sensing that the car was immobile. And I found my parents talking through the window to a family of three standing outside, asking for a ride to Turkey. We continued driving along with them.*

*The little girl looked fatigued, yet she smiled graciously at me. I smiled back and turned to glance at her mother and father. Her father seemed to be absorbed in his thoughts, but her mother looked* at me tenderly and caressed my head affectionately. When my father asked about them, they started narrating their tearjerker.

"This is my wife, and she is my daughter. We have been living in Afrin. Six months back, we lost our two sons and my parents in one of the missile attacks. On that very day, my father was watering the plants in our backyard when the first missile struck. Hearing the explosion, my mother and both my sons ran to check on him when the second missile struck, killing all of them in one blow. We both were busy putting our daughter to sleep, having us escape the attack. The missiles spared us, but the grief of losing our children and parents is still agonising for us. But at any cost, we wanted to take our daughter to a safe place. So, we determined to head for Lebanon. After much hardship and risk, we reached Lebanon. There, we suffered a lot for two months in an informal camp, after which we were deported. They threatened us to sign a form stating we requested to be sent back to Syria and disguised us as 'voluntary returns.' But we will never give up and keep trying until we reach a safe place. So, this time, we are up to Turkey."

After listening to his story, something inside me hinted that our journey would not be as easy as my father had portrayed to us. I sneaked a look at that man to check if he was crying. But he didn't. A man would cry after his first affliction, after his second and third, maybe. But even after being attacked back-to-back continuously? No, he gets hardened.

As we neared the border, people were already pouring by whatever conveyance possible: cars, trucks, buses, tractors, and carts.

When we reached that place, eventually, we had to confront the border police and the men in uniforms demanding papers. They couldn't care less about what we had left behind or who we had lost. It just doesn't matter to them. All they want are those inanimate papers.

Our passports, national identity cards, birth certificates, and everything else would have been burned to ashes this minute. A house is not just built in days. It takes years of memories and a profound emotional attachment for a building to be called a home. I witnessed the destruction of our home and all the belongings inside.

As a consequence of not having any papers they asked for, we were asked to get out of the car and join the group of people already standing there for hours. I noticed a parking lot brimming with deserted vehicles and watched my father park our car, which we had with us for around five years. I saw people ready to get out of the cursed place, even if it meant forsaking all that they had. Now, we were ready to resume our journey on foot.

When they finally allowed us inside, after hours, opening the barbed wire fence, I knew it had begun. Once I take a few more steps forward, I am exiting one life and entering another—a refugee life. It seemed to me like I had abandoned my country and left it undefended. That thought made me unintentionally fall on my knees, bend and kiss the land, the land I was born in and the land which I'm never going to see again. I got up and followed my parents, walking past the border fence into statelessness, vulnerability, insecurity, and powerlessness. My life as a refugee officially started, and I became a refugee.

From the border, we had to reach Kilis, a city near the border. It would have just taken twenty minutes by car, but we had to walk for two hours along the fields and barren lands in the cold. That was the first time in my life that I walked for hours. I huffed and puffed all the way through, and my back and legs started aching. Aqeel *walked for a short while, and my father carried him. That was when I wished to turn into a small boy again, contradicting how I always wanted to be given responsibilities and treated as a grown-up.*

*Nearing the city's outskirts, we noticed many tents, and my father turned to us, saying, "We will have to stay in tents like these for a few days. We still have a very long journey."*

*People were flocking around a refugee aid package truck on the other side of the tents. They were given bread, oil, sugar, and other basic food items. Looking at them, my father hurried to get something for us to pull through for a few days. I was shattered when I saw him returning empty-handed and with a dejected face. I have seen him helping people with money and food, and now I see him relying on someone for food.*

*I asked him, "We have money. Why don't we buy something instead of benefiting from their help?"*

*He replied, "We still have a very long journey, Wasim. We don't know when and where we ought to spend money. We don't know what we are about to face. We are not as we were in our country. We are refugees here. So, we shouldn't spend money thoughtlessly. When we could benefit from help, we have to."*

*Hearing our conversation, a man approached us and offered to stay in his house. At first, the well-built man with a big, thick moustache seemed dubious. But after he introduced himself as Mahmut, who owns a travel company in Istanbul and explained that he often helps people who come as refugees with accommodation and food. He gained our trust. Not only us, but he also took two other families with him to his farmhouse. It was a rudimentary house with cement floors and basic furniture. Four rooms were in it, and one was already occupied by a refugee family who came a week before. Mahmut also said that that house has always been occupied by refugee families for the past two years.*

*"If any of them leaves, I will bring someone new instead. I comprehend the agony you would have faced. We couldn't stand apart from it because we come from the same people. There's no difference between us," he said, asking us to get into his jeep.*

*On the way, he continued, "We used to deliver aid across the border for the people stuck there. Then, it became too dangerous. Once, when we were delivering assistance, someone on the Syrian side sprayed us with gunfire. I was wounded in the leg. One policeman was killed, and thirteen people were injured," he recalled. "But we would not stop offering help because of such incidents."*

* * *

*A few days of stay at Mahmut's house served us some breathing space to sink in what's happening in our lives and what's yet to happen. I thought how lucky we were to not stay in those dreary tents. I took advantage of imagining a not-so-complicated refugee life ahead.*

*My father decided that we must get to Ankara as soon as possible. So, after thanking Mahmut, we started to Ankara. Several people walked for almost ten days to reach Ankara. But my father opted to spend money on a taxi. Thus, we reached Adana and, from there, Ankara in nine hours.*

*The man my father had already contacted helped us find a house, almost a shanty, in an area where there were so many people who* had fled Syria, telling us that we couldn't stay in better parts of the city. He also took me along with my father to an aged person who owned a workshop, and they offered us a terrible job. We had to work for fourteen to sixteen hours a day until our backs were marred from hunching over the machine and were paid much less than the minimum wage, which was around one hundred to one hundred and fifty euros a month.

That pay was not enough for our food and to buy basic necessities. My mother and father often skipped two meals a day so that we could eat at least two meals a day. We didn't have sufficient blankets to cover ourselves. We four squash into one double blanket to escape the cold nights. My father had brought us to safety, but now he had to see us sinking into poverty.

The worst part in Turkey was that the workshop owner used to give me a small piece of cake every day, which made me believe that, though he was inconsiderate of the defenceless fugitives, at least he was able to be sympathetic to a child. I got used to eating the cake before starting work. Gradually, I realised that I was addicted to the cake, and it made me have difficulty sleeping adequately.

After a few days of self-observation and making sure about the effects, I told my father about this, who initially brushed it off, saying it might be due to the mental pressure of our situation. After about a month, I started looking tired, with bloodshot eyes and with dark half-circles under my eyes. Sometimes, I even found it difficult to breathe and eat.

This time, I told my mother about this, who took me to someone she knew at the end of our street. That family had settled in Turkey a year before. They had their daughter study medicine in Syria. However, due to the war, she could not continue her final year of studies. She examined me and doubted that those seemed like the effects of some drug intake. Straightaway, I told her about the cake and how I got addicted to it. After hearing this, the news she gave took us aback.

She apprised us of how these vicious employers abuse and exploit the refugees who work illegally by lacing foodstuffs with a drug called amphetamine, which is capable of impairing a person physically and psychologically, in an effort to keep the employees awake, energetic and focused to work for longer hours.

After learning this, my parents were distressed about continuing to stay in Turkey. Though we are extremely grateful to Turkey for taking us in and to the Turks, who are warm and welcoming, not everyone was. There is a lot of abuse and mistreatment by the locals, who want to keep us away from settling in Turkey. We had to do back-breaking work illegally for minimum wages and had to always be in fear of being sent back to the war zone again.

The Turkish government couldn't help every one of us with healthcare and education as it struggled under the burden of supporting the world's largest refugee population. Amidst these menaces and instability, Turkey no longer became a better place for us. Furthermore, the war in Syria was in full swing, with no hope to cease or decline, resulting in no prospect of being able to go home any time soon.

We needed to begin a new life in a new place. At that stage, we considered the risky journey to Europe. We have heard our people say that many European countries like Germany, France, Sweden, and Norway are helping with refugee resettlement. They also affirm that they feel welcomed and that life there is better. After dwelling on the thought, we finally started to plan the perilous journey to Europe. In *a few days, we wrapped up our bare essentials and moved towards our promised land in a bid for a new life.*

* * *

*The journey of risking death, capture, and deportation was not as easy as it seemed. We had to make many prudent choices at every step, following a big dilemma. The first one for us was to decide where to go from Turkey— Greece, or Bulgaria.*

*In terms of safety and legal protections, both countries have made efforts to improve conditions for refugees and ensure that they are able to access basic services and support. However, both countries have also faced criticism for their treatment of refugees, including reports of violence, abuse, and neglect in detention centres and at borders. Yet, Greece has a more developed legal framework for refugee protection, including a comprehensive asylum system and a legal aid system for refugees. Bulgaria, on the other hand, has been criticised for its handling of asylum claims and has been accused of forcibly returning refugees to Turkey and other countries without proper legal procedures.*

*So, Greece was our first choice. We took the train from Ankara and reached Istanbul in four and a half hours. From there, we had to take a taxi to reach Edirne, the place where one can get to Greece's border. At the Turkey-Greece border crossing, there were thousands of migrants amassed, as there was a clash with Greek police who fired tear gas to prevent us from entering. In response, some of the migrants started hurling stones at the police, which intensified the tussle.*

*This happening accounts for Turkey having its border with Greece closed so as to impede migrants and refugees from getting into the*

*European Union owing to the EU-Turkey deal. The deal was to stop people from travelling irregularly from Turkey to the Greek Islands, for which Turkey gained some benefits.*

Riya interrupted, "We couldn't bawl out at the deal like that. Turkey is the country with the most refugees in the world, as it has taken in three times as many Syrians as the whole EU. And the reason Turkey received six billion euros was as financial aid to improve the humanitarian situation faced by the vast refugee community hosted in the country. The deal's message was obvious. Of course, it was to check the enormous number of people getting into the EU illegally risking their lives. However, the EU member states contributed to accepting one Syrian refugee who waited patiently in Turkey for every Syrian sent back."

"Do you find this fair? How long? How long do we have to wait, breaking our backs and letting our eyes pop out without adequate sleep? How long do we have to let ourselves be abused? How long do we have to live without proper medical assistance and education for our children? How long should we be in fear of being sent back again to the middle of the war? Who told them Turkey was safe for us? Why? Why should we suffer? Can't the powerful EU member states sign a deal with Syria, Iraq and Israel to not wreck our homes and devastate our lives? If we had our home, why would we barge into other countries?"

"But wasn't the deal a success?" retorted Riya.

"It was. For those who bothered only about the number of irregular arrivals in Europe, it was portrayed as a success. But the figures say only a negligible amount of around 3000 Syrian refugees were transferred from Turkey to Europe while still there are more than 2.8 million Syrians currently in Turkey."

After a strong rant at Riya's defence, Wasim continued,

*Turkey had its border closed until two days before we decided to leave. Due to political considerations and a shift in migration dynamics, the then-president of Turkey opened the border with the EU for the migrants, and they weren't stopped from crossing into the EU.*

*Following Turkey's decision, Greece had to bolster its border, not letting the migrants through. In that situation, we had to choose again between either waiting in dire conditions until Greece opens its border, sleeping in the open in below-freezing conditions and struggling with food and water scarcity or taking a chance through Bulgaria.*

*As we decided to continue our journey, taking a longer detour through Bulgaria, the most harrowing thing ever in my life happened. We lost Aqeel in the crowd. We lost him forever.*

* * *

*That day, among the mass at the Turkey-Greece border, while my parents were busy discussing what to do next and I was absorbed in their conversation, we missed him. My father searched for him like a madman, shouting his name aloud and racing here and there through the crowd. My mother, who was strong enough, even when we were standing in our roofless home after the attack in Syria, was broken and sank to the ground. My father came running to me, asked me not to move away from my mother, and went further away to search for Aqeel. I stood beside my mother, stumped, hoping my father would definitely return with Aqeel. All that I could do was start praying.*

*In those two months in Turkey, Aqeel was getting stabler, gaining the ability to speak again and be normal. He was always with my mother, and we never left him alone, fearing that might hinder his improvement. So, when we missed him, my mother turned hysterical. She was repeating over and over that Aqeel had been taken back to Syria because we had heard people being duped over, luring them into the EU, through the Balkan route, and reverting to Syria by bus.*

*After an hour of searching, my father came back to us. My mother burst out, saying that those brutes had taken her child away from her. She strongly believed that Aqeel had been taken back to Syria, and she wanted to return to Syria in search of him.*

*"Take me there, please, take me back home. Let's go back to Syria. I don't want this peaceful life. How can I live peacefully without my child? I don't want to live at all, let my child live, but not in that hell. Let's go back, please. Please take me to Syria. I don't want a well-built house, I don't want a roof over the house, I can live without anything, but I can't live without my child. Please," she cried frantically.*

*I dare not see my mother's frightened eyes ever again in my life. Looking at both my parents in such a condition, an immense fear crept inside my stomach, adding burden to my heart, which was already about to explode. My perturbed father reassured her, saying he'd take her back to Syria and would find Aqeel as soon as possible.*

*He turned to me as if he had made a final decision, "Wasim, listen to me carefully. We don't have a normal life now. Our home, family, and life are ripped apart. We don't have our dear Aqeel now with us.*

*We love you both equally. I also know how much you love him. But now, your mother and I are going in search of Aqeel, and you are going to go in search of a new life."*

*After hearing this from my father, my mother shrieked, "How brutal! I already lost one, and now you are trying to lose the other," she spoke weakly.*

*My father looked at her regretfully and turned to me again, "Look, dear son. We have lost everything in the war, though we were never a part of the war. We were forced to get into the battlefield. This world is now your battlefield. As long as you are stateless, this world will treat you badly. You need to fight against them. Remember the story of the Battle of Badr, I have told you. Allah will help us. He will help the righteous. We have never wronged anyone. The world has wronged us. That doesn't mean we have to be endlessly oppressed. Go with these people. They told me that they were taking the Balkan route through Bulgaria. Follow them, and you will be able to reach Italy. Once you reach northern Italy, you are half safe. France is next to Italy. After you reach France, you can apply for refugee status, after which you can continue your studies. Finish your studies, get a good job, earn money righteously, and live a happy life. This is your only shot at a normal life. Now, you aren't just sixteen, you are just two years behind to be an adult, and that doesn't make much difference. We will somehow find Aqeel and join you there. Your mother and I will always be in your heart. Whatever confusion you get in life, ask your heart. Have this money, my card, and my phone too. Never use the money unless you are hungry or in danger. You can charge the phone wherever possible, and you know the PIN of my card," tears welled up in his eyes, and my mother was crying bitterly.*

They both hugged me, and my father's last words were, "Come on, Wasim, you are a warrior now. We love you so much," and shoved me off into the group of people who were on the way to Bulgaria.

# Chapter 7

*I didn't feel sad, I didn't feel like crying, I didn't feel like screaming out loud, I didn't feel like running away elsewhere. All I felt was empty. I felt like I had no soul in my body as I walked aimlessly for more than four hours without any break. I went over what had just happened repeatedly in my mind and was least caring to catch sight of where I was going.*

*All of a sudden, I sensed a shift in the atmosphere. The earthy scent of the damp leaves and moist soil, in tandem with the sound of the crinkling leaves and buzzing insects, awakened me to grasp where I was.*

*"We had to reach the border just at twilight," I heard someone whispering behind me as we sneaked into the forests of the Bulgarian border. Suddenly, I heard gunshots fired in the air, and everyone scattered and scampered back into Turkey's border again. A man behind me was shot, and he fell down, holding his legs in excruciating pain. I stopped for a minute but was dragged ahead by a young man. He held my hand and continued running, tugging me along. Upon reaching a safe place, he let my hand loose and sat down on the ground breathing heavily.*

*"What do you think of yourself? Do you think you could have saved him? You would have lost your life too," the young man started conversing.*

*"I thought they would just prevent us from entering. But they are shooting!" exclaimed Wasim.*

*"They will shoot you, wound you, take you to the detention centre, undress you, and will do all sorts of cruelty. They are monsters. The last time I tried crossing the border, a small girl of around four years old was shot dead in front of her mother."*

*"Last time? Is this not your first time?"*

*"This is the fifth time. I have been trying both from Greece and Bulgaria, walking back and forth every day for almost a month. Many people here are trying to cross the border for the nth number of times. Some people give up and go back, but we will not give up. We will try again tonight. The crossing is possible only during twilight and a few hours after that in the natural low light."*

*"What's your name, Akhi?" I asked him. "Hassan," he replied with a smile.*

*Till the next twilight, before sunrise, we both exchanged each other's tales of woes.*

*When it was time, all the thirty people lined up and marched towards the border. Spotting a huge tree, everyone hid behind it. One by one, we ran stealthily to the next tree and the next and next until we crossed the crucial border area. When it was Hassan's turn, he turned back to me and asked me to go first. That look in his eyes was so intense and conveyed that he wanted me to cross the border safely. I couldn't say no to him and at once sprinted.*

*Once I reached the last tree, I didn't want to hurry and join the others. So, I waited there until Hassan joined me. When he arrived at the first tree and was on the way to the second, alas! We saw a flashlight flashing around. It was the Bulgarian border police who were on the night shift. Hassan swiftly lay down flat on the ground. As the light verged on, pointing on all random sides, my heart started racing, and I couldn't breathe for a few minutes. I amassed my entire focus on Hassan, supplicating that the light doesn't fall on him.*

*After a few minutes, the police, who did just their routine, left when they didn't find anything suspicious. And Hassan came running to me without stopping at any of the trees. We both hugged each other, and the moment yielded an emotion of unidentified bonding that had already developed between us.*

* * *

*Once in Bulgaria, we stopped in the thick of the pine forest to catch some breath after hours of crucial crossing and also agreed to get further into the country in the next two or three days. But dismally, it exceeded a week so as not to be detected by the border authorities. Some members of the group were well-prepped with camping gear, tents, and blankets. Nonetheless, a few of us, including Hassan and I, were bound to sleep outside in the open air, shivering in the biting cold. In the later part of the night, when the crisp, cold air touch my body, my skin breaks out in goosebumps. While each wave of shiver swept through my body, I instinctively curled myself and held tight to my numb toes. Furthermore, that was the first time I slept on rough and uneven ground. In fact, I didn't sleep. I just let my body repose.*

*During the day, we search for places to sleep at night—behind rocks, between two trees, or sometimes we dig trenches. Most of the time, we starved. Sometimes, we got to eat some fruits from the forest and share them with others. Due to the scarcity of food and proper sleep, my health deteriorated, and I started having headaches often. I was not able to stand upright due to hunger. All we could do was drink lots of water from a stream to protect us from starvation.*

* * *

*Finally, we were ready to leave the forest. One man in our group charged his phone using a power bank and used GPS to find the nearest village. As we were all famished, we planned to get something to eat there in the first place. Unlucky us! What we got there was not something to eat, but only a letdown. The border police had intimidated the people living near the border to immediately expose any refugees they saw inside their village. So, the villagers informed the police about us, and the Bulgarian police took us in a van to the detention centre. I asked one of those authorities if they would provide us with food there, to which he replied yes. I believed being in a detention centre with a full stomach would be better than living liberally in a forest with an empty stomach.*

*The detention centre was a big, fenced hall crammed with people and guarded by a handful of cops. We were pushed into the hall, and the gates were closed. After a while, they took us to another room, where they stripped us naked under the pretext of searching and took all our belongings. The money, card, and phone my father* gave me were confiscated. We were left naked for hours in the room. The dehumanising experience of being stripped of our clothes left us feeling vulnerable and violated, having a lasting impact on our sense of dignity and self-worth. The hours spent in that room, exposed and helpless, only intensified our desperation, making us feel like we had lost all control over our own bodies. The power and authority took not only our clothes but also our rights and humanity without any consequences.

We fled our country fearing death, but I realised that death with dignity is better than life with humiliation.

Later, they asked us to get dressed and sent us back to the hall again. We stayed there for days and weeks. For the first few nights, I had been standing and squatting for hours due to a lack of space, then managed to secure a small space where I could lie down scrunched up. There were very few toilets which were not cleaned properly. We didn't get toothpaste, brush, or soap to maintain proper hygiene. But one good thing was that our stomachs weren't fully empty. It was half-filled during the detention stay.

Without proper sanitation and enough food, many fell sick. Among them was a girl of Aqeel's age, and she reminded me of him. She was struck down with the flu for the past couple of days. Enduring body aches, diarrhoea, and vomiting for one whole day, the poor little girl got dehydrated. Her mother took the exhausted girl in her hands and begged the officials for her medical treatment. After a few hours, she was taken to the hospital and returned the next day. Seeing the girl still tired and not strong yet, my heart trembled. But no matter how many hearts tremble, this vicious world is not going to stop its atrocities.

*After thirty-five days in the detention centre, we were finally let out free. Lucky us, we got our belongings and money from the Bulgarian police when they released us. Another positive thing about this detention stay was that the centre was in Sofia. So, we didn't have to walk a long way to the capital of Bulgaria.*

* * *

*Among the thirty of us, Hassan, I, and five other people decided to go through Serbia. So, the others split and went their way. Surviving in the detention centre for many days added to our stiff limbs. After a laborious walk for a few minutes, we happened on a concrete storm tunnel under a highway. Hence, we gaily entered, lay down inside, and rolled over until our hands and legs became flexible. We slept for hours and hours, not minding our hungry stomachs. Then we woke up to clean ourselves and our clothes, using the stagnant water. Later, we walked towards the city centre to find something to eat.*

*I didn't understand what was going on in my life. I was done figuring out what was wrong with us. Why does everyone derogate and devalue us? Doesn't this world realise we are dying to live? You have ripped off basic respect, safety, shelter, and sustenance from us. You will have to answer for your actions and remember you may not be shown mercy then.*

*The Bulgaria-Serbia border route was not an easy one. With the rugged terrain, it was difficult to navigate, especially when we were not familiar with the route. Attempting to cross on our own may result in arrest or detention again, as the security measures have been increased along the border and additional guards have been deployed. So, we chose to use the services of smugglers. Though they were a bit* expensive, we would at least not get lost in the wilderness and not risk being caught by authorities.

From a person in the detention centre, we were given the contact information of a migrant smuggler operating along the Balkan route. We contacted him and met at a coffee shop. He asked us to deposit 2,000 euros each in Western Union before he would take us over a remote stretch of mountains into Serbia.

I remembered what my father had told me. Now that I was neither in danger nor in hunger, I was reluctant to spend the money on a smuggler. While all others had got it done, my father's words echoed inside me making me more unwilling to pay the smuggler.

Hassan came forward and encouraged me to believe—to believe others and to not doubt everyone. He said that the one deceived would be at fault, not the one who had suffered. For some reason, his words paralleled with my father's frequently given advice to my mother. So, I decided to do it too. After having done the transaction, we walked through the night on a carefully chosen track set up by the network of smugglers and made it to Serbia.

Unfavourably, Croatia had closed its border with Serbia, Hungary, and Slovenia to keep the inflow of migrants in check and had also enforced various border control measures. Consequently, we were stranded in the refugee camp near the Serbia-Croatia border with no hope of figuring out a way. Back to square one: cramped tents with ten to twelve people, inadequate food and water, pathetic hygiene maintenance, and poor medical assistance. Adding to the list, there were restrictions on moving freely, which made things complicated. Granted that we managed to leave the camp, we had to fear abuse and violence outside of it.

"Have you ever seen a refugee camp?" asked Wasim at Riya. When she said no, he showed some pictures taken in the camp.

*"Muddy tents on gravelly ground, one water tank for ten to twenty tents, women cooking outside with minimal groceries, and kids, who once got to have any toy they wished, are now playing around with either nothing or whatever secondhand toys they get. Look at them, at each of their faces. Could you imagine how they would have lived in their homes? They slept on cosy beds in their bedrooms, cooked in their well-equipped kitchens, and maintained proper hygiene in their sophisticated bathrooms. Let alone the tedious chores and dearth of luxury, we treat our women as queens, but now their dignity, safety, and privacy are nowhere to be found. They struggle to make it through each day, scraping through family separation, psychological stress, trauma, and health conditions without an emotional support network. It's a disaster."*

As it's said, "Every cloud has a silver lining," the nice side of being in a camp was that there were thousands of Syrian people: aged, young men and women, teens like me, children and babies. We were like family there. For those who lost their father, there are fathers who lost their children. For those who lost their mother, there are mothers who lost their children. For those who lost their siblings, there are a number of brothers and sisters. We had grandparents, fathers, mothers, brothers, sisters and plenty of friends. Not one, but many. We sit together and talk over a lot of topics: food, sports, automobiles, family, local affairs, international politics, news updates, and much about how tranquil and enchanting Syria was before.

*One night in the camp, an elderly man sitting under a lamppost was looking at something passionately inside his hand. I went behind him and peered to see a small piece of postal stamp.*

*When I asked him about it, "This is an old Syrian postal stamp. Our country was this beautiful," he replied and wiped his tears.*

*"Can I take a look at it?" I asked.*

*"Certainly, young man. The younger generation should know how our country was. But, please be careful, even though they are worthless now."*

*I took it in my hand and noticed how astonishingly beautiful it was.*

*"Isn't this the Khalid ibn al-walid mosque?" I asked.*

*"Yes, it is. Have you been there?" he questioned.*

*"Just once, when I was too small. I don't remember much. Once, my father said that it had been damaged in the war," I recounted.*

*And he started narrating, "Yes, it has been extensively marred. The beautiful powder blue coloured central dome, surrounded by a few smaller domes and minarets, towered up from the enfolded landscape and created a striking silhouette against the sky. When you enter the central prayer hall through the arched doorway and feel the rays of skylight illuminating the entire place, it's pure bliss. Do you even know what plight it is in now? The beautiful domes are tarnished with broken, soiled spots all over, as a result of the strikes and bombardments. The frosty white walls are stained with ashes of the smouldering fire. The intricate designs are deformed, and the glass windows and chandeliers are shattered. The entire place is covered by remains and debris of the damaged parts," he remained silent for a few seconds.*

*The old man continued, "Now, it's totally in a terrible state. Not only the mosque but the entire country is bearing the marks of the ongoing destruction. Our country has shown its history and culture through its architecture and infrastructure, which have now turned into ruined structures and are unrecognizable. The once vibrant country with sophisticated architecture; each building in different shades of gold, is now tainted with traces of grey and black. The magnificent landscape made up of lush greenery is now arid and full of ashes and lots of sand. Busy roads swarming with cars and vans are now replaced with military troops and artillery tanks. Syria is gone now. It doesn't exist anymore."*

*He went on without stopping, "Have you seen the Aleppo Souk? The bustling stretch of bazaars was with vivid lights all along, various colourful clothes, jewellery, and other handicrafts stacked in front of each store. It always used to be lively with vendors calling out and customers bargaining. But now, horrendous. They have been reduced to rubbles, and the complete area has been cluttered with remnants and shattered pieces of bricks and glass. The eerie silence inside is broken by the echoing sound of gunfire and explosion every now and then."*

*He held the upper tip of his nose, shrinking his eyes, and suddenly, he started tremoring with a loud yelp before continuing, "Everything in my country is precious to me. But what a catastrophe it is to witness the destruction of everything I hold dear at this age!" he sighed with tears rolling down his wrinkled and sagged cheeks.*

*"After having lost my family, I didn't want to live at my home without my wife. So, without any preparation, I left for Turkey. After four years of hardship in Turkey, I met a migrant smuggler who promised to send me to the United Kingdom. He took all the money I had and also made me leave the thawb I was wearing and gave me a T-shirt and pants to look more European and not to stick out and attract attention. After I had given everything I possessed, the only things I was able to take with me were my wedding ring, which mattered most to me, my Syrian ID and these stamps that remind me of when my country was safe."*

# Chapter 8

*After failing at all nine attempts to enter Croatia, as our tenth attempt, we gathered information from a trafficker that a tanker was entering the Croatian border. Its driver regularly helps migrants pass through countries for a sum of money. We, a group of thirteen boys, managed to slip out of the camp and approached the tanker parked on a side lane. One of us met the driver and brought him near the tanker.*

*The driver was keen on getting money from us first. Then, he briefed us that he was taking hot liquid chocolate from Greece to Croatia and would select only the five tallest ones among us so we didn't get drowned inside the deep tanker. He also warned us that we would lose our money if we changed our minds in the middle. As I was desperate to leave the country and didn't care even if I died inside the tank, I agreed. Favourably, both Hassan and I were among the five, and the other eight had left grieving.*

*He instructed us to hide in the forest area and get into the tanker while on the road between the first checkpoint and the second. Just as he directed, we got into the tanker through the hatch while it was waiting in the long queue and waited inside for thirty minutes for him to cross the border and halt the vehicle in a safe place, hoping for a better life soon.*

*Once we got inside, we were covered in warm chocolate up to a few centimetres under our necks. At first, being covered in warm and velvety chocolate was fascinating. However, after a few minutes, we started feeling uncomfortable and had difficulty breathing. It was like all the air was sucked out and was getting hotter and hotter inside. I felt like I was being boiled alive. We decided to bear it, as we knew it was going to last only for a few more minutes, and we would move on to the next step in our journey to a better life.*

*But after a long while, the tanker didn't seem to move, and it's been more than an hour. We then realised that the driver had said it would take twenty minutes once the tanker started moving, but the tanker hadn't started moving yet. At that moment of crunch, I started hallucinating like I was slowly submerging in the chocolate. I tried to flail my hands as if trying to swim, but I couldn't move them freely as the chocolate was very sticky and heavy. I struggled to keep my head above the chocolate with my mouth open, trying to gasp for air. And there I started crying, wanting to leave.*

*As the heat was terrible, everyone agreed to leave. Since the hatch was not locked for our safety, one of us opened it from inside and helped me get out. It would have been unmanageable to get out of the viscous liquid without someone pushing us out from inside. Thus, the last person, Fadel, struggled to get himself out, as there was no one to push him from inside. We all tried harder to pull him out, but the chocolate was sucking him inside, and our grips slipped from his hand. He almost drowned. But we tried over and over, and finally, he came out free, but his shoes were left behind. Breathing a sigh of relief, we walked back to our tents with chocolate covered all over us.*

* * *

That night, I was sitting outside of our tent, reminiscing about how my father used to buy us imported chocolates and how Aqeel and I relished those. Life has now thrown me into a state where I would never enjoy chocolates.

Later that night, while I was still outside, Fadel came near and sat next to me.

"How do you feel now?" he asked.

"The way this brain thinks is weird. At that moment, I wanted to break open the tanker and rush out to save my life, but now I regret not having been dead inside," I complained.

"There's death all around us. Each day in the life of a refugee is on par with death. That being the case, we neither have to fear death nor wish for it," he lectured.

I cowered down, closing my face with my hands, and cried out aloud to my father, "Baba, please come and save me. Take this pain away from me. It's more than I can bear." Suddenly, I was reminded of Aqeel. "What if he is also suffering like me? Then, Baba has to save him first," I was stuck in this mental battle.

Fadel hugged me from the side, trying to console me, "Things get harder before you level up. Remember that you have been saved up from an enormous ordeal. This shows that you are more powerful than you think."

"I have never considered myself powerful," I subdued.

"At times, even to live is an act of courage and sign of power," he said.

"What's the point? I might be powerful. Every single person in this camp is powerful. But, we all combined together become powerless before this ruthless world."

"We don't belong here, Wasim. So, we can't be stuck here forever. Life will definitely change. And you, never underestimate your power. That will take your life in a new direction. We've been through difficult times in Syria, and it's taught us to never give up."

I started contemplating what he was saying.

He continued, "This night. Your pain will fade. Your story will change. Your life will get better."

"This night," I laughed and asked, "What if it doesn't?"

"I'll come tomorrow and say this again. I will say this every day until that night. One night, your life will change for certain."

We laughed together, and Fadel began to spurt out his story of how he is responsible for finding a new home in a new country for his family, who is relying on him and waiting in Turkey. After losing everything in the war and selling the remaining properties for a fraction of their value, Fadel fled to Turkey with his pregnant wife and a two-year-old daughter. Leaving them there in safety, he joined the drill.

He always said, "This is for the sake of my daughters. My wife is pregnant once again; we'd already seen the ultrasound scan in Turkey, and another girl is on the way. I left Syria so that I could get them out of this war and provide a secure life. I risk my future for theirs and endure all these for them. I am ready to die if they could live safely. But before providing them safety, I'm never going to quit."

* * *

*At this point in time, a large chunk of the money given by my father has been spent. After three months of waiting in the camp, we went to the internet cafe to try connecting with our families. That is the place where a lot of Syrian youths drop in to use the internet facility. While all the others were speaking with their parents and siblings, and some were still trying to connect with them, I was standing alone, thinking of my parents and Aqeel.*

*I thought to myself, "Where did everyone go? Where are they now? They would have found Aqeel, and they might be together. At least Aqeel should be with our parents, which is why I am striving alone here." I felt vulnerable, and I wanted myself, as well, to be safe with my parents as much as I wanted Aqeel to be. Though I was becoming an adult, I missed the caress and cuddles from my parents. I missed being treated fairly. I was sick of being helpless and standing alone.*

*I noticed something strange and later learned that the cafe owner was a migrant smuggler and the cafe was just a front for the smuggling operation. He would nose around to get to know who of us were trying to get into Western Europe. He identified us too and proposed to take us to Italy for a three-thousand-euro deposit per person. I knew Hassan didn't possess so much money, and I couldn't give up on him to go forward in this journey. So, I turned down the proposal and was about to leave when Hassan stopped me and told the smuggler that we would give some thought to it and get back to him later that day, asking him to wait in a nearby park.*

*"Akhi, I know you don't have that much money. I also assume that you are trying to send me with him. But you better know I ain't going any forward in this journey leaving you behind," I rebuked.*

"Wasim, remember what your father told you? We are on the battlefield. There is no space for emotions and sentiments. You better reach France as soon as possible and wait for your family to join you. I have no one to live for in this world. If I had someone now, it would be you. That's why I want you to get going. Be ready. We will meet the smuggler in the evening and negotiate the deal for three-fourths of what he proposed because all you have is three thousand euros now. And you can't spend the entire money on this. You still need to thrive until you reach France, apply for asylum, and get refugee status," he tried convincing me.

That evening, when we met the smuggler in the park, Hassan drove a hard bargain and made him accept to take me to Italy for two thousand five hundred euros. When they were up to close the deal, I barged in and told the smuggler that we would give him the three thousand euros he asked for and begged him to take Hassan and Fadel along. Fadel gushed that he had some money and put forward that they would give five thousand five hundred in total to take the three of us, which the smuggler regrettably refused.

I cried, saying we'll take up any job once we reach Italy and pay him the remaining money. Though the smuggler turned me down, he prompted us to work and earn the money needed, right there in Serbia. He also offered to introduce us to someone who can give us work illegally. Turning a deaf ear to Hassan, I accepted the smuggler's offer.

"I'm sorry, Akhi. But are you ready to work? Let's go to Italy together," I asked Hassan with a beaming smile.

He smiled back and gently ran his hand through my hair.

* * *

*The next day when the smuggler was taking us in his car to a construction site, Hassan looked at me and asked, "Why do you look anxious ?"*

*"I don't know, akhi. Maybe because of the past unpleasant working experience back in Turkey" I replied.*

*"Don't fret. I won't let anything happen to you this time. Now calm yourself down" he cheered me up.*

*The smuggler took us to an older man who was the builder of the site. They both talked for a while, making us wait a little farther, after which the smuggler left. The old man came to us and asked for our details.*

*"We are from Syria. We are trying to reach a safe place from where we can call upon our family whom we have left in the middle of the battlefield. We didn't have enough money to pay the smuggler who offered to take us to Italy. So, if we could earn some money by working here for a few months, we will be able to continue our journey," briefed Fadel.*

*"What kind of job do you know, young men?" he asked.*

*"Sir, back in Syria, my only job was going to school to study and spend time with my beautiful family. Now that I neither have my family nor anything to study, I am ready to do any job you give me," I answered.*

*The old man was stirred with emotions and asked, "What were you studying in Syria?"*

*"He was in secondary school, and I was studying architecture at Damascus University," responded Hassan.*

The old man came near us, patted me on my back and said, "Usually, for refugees who want to work illegally, I give only half of what I give to legal workers. Because when I hire undocumented workers, I'm prone to face major fines and penalties. In that case, I can pay you 25 euros per person daily. And your work will be physically demanding. Is that ok for you?"

"How long should we work in a day?" I asked.

"From nine in the morning till five in the evening is the rule," he replied.

"Sir, we don't want to waste our time. Five to six hours of sleep a day is enough for us, and we are willing to work in the remaining time," I requested.

"No, no, no. I can't do that to anyone. I have my morales," he said strictly.

Looking at our dejected faces, he asked Hassan if he would draw architectural plans for his next project. And he mentioned that only if he likes the plan will he pay for it.

Along with the job, he gave us food daily and a decent place to stay within the construction site. After working there for two months doing odd jobs and running errands, Fadel and I managed to earn a thousand five hundred euros. Along with that amount, Hassan also earned an extra six hundred euros for the plans he drew.

Sometimes, life amazes you with a miracle. And it comes from people who are good at heart. Nikola was the reason a miracle happened in our life after a great deal of affliction.

# Chapter 9

*We contacted the smuggler again, and he asked us to prepare for a long journey for the next few days through land and water. Apprised of the perils, we bought life jackets, blankets, and some food for the journey ahead. Fadel bought a pair of shoes as he lost them in the chocolate tanker.*

*Looking at Hassan buying balloons in the shop, I was surprised and asked him what he would do with them.*

*He remembered, "After my first attempt to Europe, I was sent back to a refugee camp in Turkey where I met a man who shared his experience. When he was trying to reach Greece through the Aegean Sea, his boat was captured by the coastguard. To escape from them, he jumped into the water, but unfortunately, he got caught and was detained. All the money he had saved got drenched and damaged.*

*He gave me this tip to keep money safely by putting them into the rubber balloons if I had to cross the sea."*

*Hassan bought three balloons, one for each. He safely put his money inside and inserted it into his jacket's inner pocket.*

* * *

The next evening, the smuggler met us in a park to inform us, "Due to the strict restrictions of illegal migrants, we can't sneak you in by land. All the vehicles are being checked and scanned scrupulously. So, it is difficult in trucks and tankers."

With a sigh of relief, I replied, "We wouldn't want it either."

"What's the plan?" asked Hassan seriously.

"From Sid, we will take you by car to a small tourist town that sits along the Danube River. As many tourists frequent there, we have the slightest chance to look unusual. There is a vast natural reserve bordering the town. You will have to travel through the forest until you reach the river. And then cross the river to the other side where there is a small piece of land, a disputed territory between the two countries, the Liberland. Neither of the countries have officially recognized it. That is our only way out. This is a route drawn up for the first time by our network members. You are going to give it an attempt. If you fail, you carry the load. But, if you succeed, it will be a passage out for many desperate stranded refugees like you."

"But, how can we navigate through the wilderness?" demanded Fadel.

"No need to sweat about the national reserve. There is a local guide waiting in the town to steer you. Nevertheless, the river and Liberland are your responsibility. After confirming that there are no police activities, you walk an hour more to Zmajevac. There you meet another member of us," said the smuggler and asked us to jot down the second smuggler's number.

*I was a little sceptical about this plan and his arrangements. What if he left us abandoned? But before Fadel and I could contemplate it, Hassan agreed.*

*"Considering the fact that we had to build a supplementary network and connect with many people, we want you to give six hundred euros in addition to what we had agreed upon," the smuggler claimed.*

*"I am sorry, but we can't believe anyone without assurance. We will give the money, but, after reaching Italy, to the person who will take us there," guaranteed Hassan.*

*After finishing the deal and taking the person's number, we got into the smuggler's car. We drowsed well throughout the three-hour journey and woke up with fresh minds willing to face new adventures. Without stopping over anywhere, we entered a riverside coffee shop. Acting like tourists, we four had coffee and some snacks till dusk, after which the smuggler left, and the guide joined us to take us through the forest. We walked along the bank of a small canal for a few miles and crossed it over a fragile, narrow bridge entering the national reserve zone.*

*As we entered, the distant lights from the village stopped giving their contribution to us. If not for the moon, it would have been pitch-dark. Moreover, a trekking path was already out there, so we didn't have to tread upon prickly shrubs and thorny bushes. The guide was clammed up all the way through until we swerved and went off track for around two kilometres.*

*"This portion of the forest has limited access to human activities. Be cautious and look out for wild boars. Just a few more minutes, and we will reach the river," he cautioned us.*

*We were taken aback by that. But for some reason, I still had hope that we would safely make it to the river. I walked with my arms crossed over my chest so as to defend myself from the cold and wilderness.*

*After a while, I sensed a mild needle prick on the side of my neck. At first, I thought it might be the plants brushing against me. Then, I felt something moving in that place. Once I touched and realised something was on me, I quickly tried to push it aside, but it didn't fall off. I bounced and hollered in fright and revulsion. The guide came running back and rebuked me for making noise. He pulled the creature sucking my blood and threw it away. Then, he plucked a leaf and placed it on my neck to stop the blood flow.*

*He said, "It's a leech, and it is common here." I was traumatized, though it was nothing in front of the massive tank artilleries.*

*We reached the shoreline of the river. The calm water with mild ripples tranquillized our souls to a slight extent. The guide showed us a tiny raft, which he had already set up, and took leave. We were left all alone in the midst of the forest. It was still the hours of darkness, and we were procrastinating our next step. For the next half hour, we sat on the edge of the river bank. We let our legs sit inside the flowing water, trying to familiarise ourselves with the coolness before we got in.*

*Tossing the raft into the water, we climbed upon it one after another. The raft was a bit brittle and not so compact for three people, yet we fitted ourselves within it. As the current favoured us, we floated effortlessly for a while. The moment we thought this journey was not going to be laborious, we heard some voices above us on the shore.*

*The river ran low and the embankment was elevated from the water level. Hence, we could hardly see anyone from the raft. We could only hear more and more voices and guessed there might be around six to ten people. We were aware that it was still Croatia's side's river bank and we were yet to reach the Liberland.*

*Warying not to run the risk of being caught by the Croatian cops, Hassan held tight to a coarse piece of rock hanging overhead along the river bank. He balanced his legs firmly on the raft to prevent it from moving further. Fadel and I pulled together doing the same, and that helped the raft position standstill. Enduring the aching hands and legs for a long time made my body numb. I was not able to bear it anymore and lost control. As I plopped down to the raft again, the other two lost balance, letting the raft move out.*

*Petrified, we slowly got into the water from the raft one by one without any ruckus and swam towards the fringe of the river, leaving the raft afloat. Along the side of the moonlit river, the soil at the bank's base had eroded, creating an overhanging ledge roofed by the soft clay soil. There, we spotted a hideout shrouding behind a damp boulder. We swam stealthily to the undercut bank, which we knew could be hazardous, causing injury or even death.*

*We three crammed ourselves inside and didn't speak a word. It had been nearly an hour, and we started struggling to breathe. Squeezed inside a narrow space, my whole body started cramping, and I was scared that I was about to black out. I shut my eyes tight, clenched my fist and remained silent but screamed inside. I screamed again and again. When I opened my eyes, the pressure released a few teardrops out.*

*Having noticed it, Fadel took out his mobile, dimmed the brightness, and kept looking at the photos of his wife and daughter.*

*He talked to himself, "I have kids. I don't want to die leaving them alone. How would they survive if I didn't make it? My second baby girl is on the way. I wonder if God would keep me alive to see the baby." He was looking at them throughout until the battery died.*

*Finally, after some time, the voices began to fade away. We were relieved to know that the patrol police had left. We scrambled ourselves out of the hideout with all speed to see that our raft was missing. But it was not possible for us to delay any longer as dawn was approaching. It became crucial for us to arrive at the Liberland before the twilight hours ended. With that in mind, we decided to go swimming all the way. After swimming a little longer, at a subsequent time, we saw the fence on the bank end, and the adjacent portion of the land remained unfenced. We rejoiced and swam even faster. Stopping near a big rock, we climbed up and stepped into Liberland.*

*Liberland is nothing but a small area on the western bank of the Danube River between Croatia and Serbia. Citing the dispute between the two countries, it has been claimed as a new country. It's a free republic with neither a formal government and law enforcement nor legal inhabitation of people, as it is not officially recognised.*

*Crossing that parcel of land would have taken an hour or two, but we took around six hours to exit that piece of land. In fact, we didn't want to because Liberland is a land of liberty. There were no army and troops to drive us away, there was no horror of being killed or losing our loved ones, and we didn't have to dread the bombings, shootings, and other acts of violence. There was peacefulness around* us. The always-existing inner turmoil and restlessness had stayed away.

The few hours we spent there were when we breathed freedom and serenity in the air after a really long time. We were free enough to enjoy the beauty of nature. We sat down under a big tree and talked for hours without any sense of foreboding. We laughed, we reminisced about our past, and we slept peacefully. It was a good break from our recent arduous lives.

Eventually, we walked towards where the smuggler asked us to go. Before reaching him, we called the person whose number was given to us by the smuggler. He picked us up in a truck and took us straight to Umag within seven hours.

* * *

Not long after that, we were dropped in a secluded place on the shore of the Adriatic Sea, which serves as the natural border between Croatia and Italy and told to wait until the dinghy came. I was standing on the flax-gold beach, looking at the sweeping sea and the cloudy distant lands ahead of me. Though the sea looked serene that day, suppressing its rumbles and murmurs, I couldn't hold back my grief.

My heart suddenly throbbed, bringing back the remembrances of my parents and Aqeel. I really missed the times in Syria with my family. Everything has been ruined and smashed to nothingness. Why should we suffer for somebody else's actions? Their hatred for each other is nothing in front of the love we share. If you could see my inner feelings outside, you would see my whole body blazing in fire, my eyes red as blood, and my mouth fuming fire. I was raging inside in silence. I had no idea where Aqeel and my parents were. I comprehended that I was standing disabled while they were at stake.

Just then, the waves did their bit by oozing onto the beach, touching my legs, and soothing my agony. Before I could see a dinghy come bobbing and lolling in the incoming tide, I saw another group of people nearing us. After dividing us into two groups, we hopped onto the two inflatable dinghies. It was overloaded, but we had to bear the risk.

A small boat with a capacity of eight people carried fifteen of us. The heaps of waves steadily tossed the boats up and down. As we went every inch forward in the desolate sea towards the faraway kingdoms, hoping for a better life, there existed forever fear of suffering, fear of abuse, fear of agony, and above all, the fear of not being able to fix the broken and shattered family. What's good in establishing a new, pleasant life when I don't have my family along to appreciate it?

Meanwhile, a woman in her late twenties started singing a song aloud. Her face was lifeless with her eyes fixed on the waving water. However, her voice precisely reflected the deep meaning of the song with all the emotions and passion. Though she appeared detached from this world, her voice didn't fail to connect with the listeners emotionally.

(Arabic song translated into English)

> We had a nice past but it has gone
>
> Got scattered in the wind, in the outdoors
>
> Still, there are memories of what happened
>
> Like the food we shared and the contentment

*Every night and day,*

*I see my life passing before my eyes*

*Everyone stopped talking and remained silent. Throughout the song, we delved deep and buried ourselves in our own thoughts, bearing in mind our lost loved ones. When I asked her about the song, she said nothing but took a CD out from her bag and showed it to me. It was the album 'Yes There is Hope' by Fairouz, one of the most famous singers in the Middle East.*

*She then started speaking, "I had to flee Syria five months after my engagement. My fiancé's family and mine planned to have our wedding the next month. That week, during a non-stop air strike, every single thing in my life was down and out: my parents, my family, my home, and my entire city, except my fiancé, Umar. He was alive, alive for me. Just as it seemed like fortunate things happened to me, something came along to ruin it.*

*A group of my relatives were leaving for Lebanon, and I was obligated to join them. I wanted to take Umar with me. But he refused. He refused, indicating that he had his parents to look after and take care of. He promised me that he would join me after having his parents settled in a safe place. Giving me this CD, he kissed me on my forehead and bid me farewell. That was the last kiss, last meet and last goodbye.*

*For five months, I stayed back in Syria at one of the border camps, trying to contact him. I didn't want to go any further away from him. I informed my relatives that I would stay in the camp or go back to Syria and die. I tried contacting him. I kept on trying. I didn't know where he was. I was scared, very scared. All the people dearest to me have been killed. No one is left except Umar. After reaching out to one of my neighbours, who still stays in Syria, I came to know that Umar was taken along with his car by the soldiers a few days before, accusing him of trying to deliver food to the people in hiding. She also managed to send me his missing person's report. While parting, I refused to go without him and told him I was afraid I would end up alone. In the end, that's what happened. I'm alone now. I prefer to go back home in search of him, but that's not an option. The only thing I could do now was sing the song, hoping that I would see him again one day, get married to him and live a peaceful life."*

*All of a sudden, from a few miles away from the shore, our boat struggled as it couldn't handle so many people. Panic kicked in, and the boat was on the brink of capsizing. Only nine people, including the three of us in the boat, were wearing life jackets. There were still six, among whom there were elderly people, ladies, and a kid without any lifeguards. Hassan and Fadel swiftly jumped into the water to reduce the load of the boat, but still holding onto it. I and another man lent our jackets to the kid and her mother. Meanwhile, the other boat which was moderately bigger, came to the rescue.*

*Along with Hassan and Fadel, two other men jumped in to drag the damaged boat near the other one and kept it holding until people got transferred. Unfortunately, we lost four members of our boat during the transfer process, including the woman who sang, and we had to move forward while we watched them struggle and drown deep down the sea. Despite witnessing the desperate struggle of those left behind, we had no choice but to continue our journey, haunted by their haunting cries.*

Ten minutes after moving to the other boat, we were in a crucial state. The boat overflowed with people, and everyone was frightened to death. So, as the depth reduced, a few of us with life jackets plunged into the water again and held the boat as it flowed.

As we verged the coast of Italy, we saw people standing ready and waiting on the coast wearing orange safety jackets. They located us and perceived that we were in distress. Some of them came running up to the shallow part of the sea, and two of them reached us in a fishing boat. They helped us into their boat and assisted us in beaching our boat.

A heap of life jackets that saved our lives were forsaken on the ground. Seeing that, I took one as a remembrance of this part of the journey. A girl approached me and asked what I was going to do with that now that I was on land.

When I told her about my intention, she asked, "What if it could help one more migrant to live?"

I noticed that she didn't use the word refugee, which pleased me. I dropped the jacket down and started talking to her. "Who are you? I didn't know that there are people who are ready to help us publicly."

She smiled and replied, "We are members of an Italian NGO. We are here to protect you, provide food and shelter, and guide you through all the procedures required. We are your friends."

"If people like you were in Syria, we would not have had to leave our country, lose our family, and endure afflictions."

"There are NGOs in Syria who provide assistance, food, shelter, and medical care to those who are affected by the ongoing conflict, in *which many of them were targeted and killed. For that very reason, you can't have them for everyone to see. However, they are still working on it. They are still rescuing and supporting people."*

*I scoffed, "There's no bias. Helpers-helpless, men-women, aged-newborns and sometimes the unborn. Everyone gets killed. Are you capable of contacting any of them?"*

*"Maybe, I can. And may I ask why?"*

*"My eight-year-old younger brother has been lost in Edirne, Turkey, when we were trying to cross the border. Guessing that he has been taken back to Syria, my parents have gone in search of him, asking me to continue the journey all alone. It has been nearly a year, and I haven't heard anything about them. Since my mother had missed her phone among the ruins after our home was attacked, and my father gave his phone to me, I am stuck not being able to contact them. I don't even know where they are. I am restless to know if they have found my brother."*

*"I know how you feel. That must be incredibly hard. But there are many people here who have lost their loved ones. We can help the people who reach this place, but nothing beyond that. Perhaps I'd let you know if I happen to see any of your family in Italy, provided that I have their picture. But only if you don't mind sharing it with me."*

*"Why would I mind? All I want now is my family. Standing all alone in an unknown country, not knowing what to do next, is like a nightmare. Never mind, this is my family," and I showed a beautiful picture of us together on my phone.*

*"Can you send it to me? This is my number," she pointed out one in a card of more than ten phone numbers."*

*I sent the picture to her and saved her number. There was not a single day that I didn't check if I had received any message from her until I lost my mobile phone at the French camp. That day in the stadium, I mistook you for her and…*

"That makes sense", interrupted Riya, not letting him explain the situation all again.

*Hassan and Fadel, who were occupied, talking with the other rescuers, called out to me. I took leave of her and walked towards them. Fadel suggested that we could stop our journey in Italy and settle down there instead of risking our lives further and further.*

*"But from what they said, I understand that that would be a temporary solution because the asylum procedures in Italy are lengthy and complicated. In addition, the support and assistance of both government and non-governmental organisations are inadequate. It is better to get to a country where there is better social inclusion and offers a degree of support to asylum seekers and provides migrants with a chance of finding work," said Hassan.*

*"Wherever you go, you are a refugee, and you are going to live through this. Who guarantees you a better life in France? There are still people who have not received refugee status and face deprivation in France. Not only in France but also in many countries. And some people have settled peacefully in Italy," retorted Fadel.*

*"What do you say, Wasim?" asked Hassan*

*"I don't know all these details. My father asked me to go to France and said he would join me there. Therefore, I have to be there waiting for them," I replied.*

*I said that ten years back. It's been a decade now, and I'm still waiting. I have failed to find them. I tried using all the online platforms and databases, social media, refugee agencies, and humanitarian organisations. But nothing worked my way.*

Following a few minutes of silence, Riya asked, "What happened then? Where are Hassan and Fadel?"

*From there, we were taken to the reception centres, where we were provided with temporary accommodation and food. After the registration and screening procedures, we decided to stay there for a few days and continue our journey to France. There, we talked with many people, both migrants and some volunteer workers of NGOs, to gather the needed information.*

*After a month in Italy, we split up with Fadel. He took a train to Munich, Germany and then to Stockholm, Sweden. As soon as he had been granted asylum and found a job, he sent for his family, whom he had left back in Turkey, through the family reunification program. They arrived in Sweden carrying a newcomer to the family, the baby girl Fadel feared he'd never see. We just came back into contact three years ago, and he sent some pictures of them together. And Hassan is married and lives here in France. They have a beautiful 4-year-old daughter.*

Riya noticed a small smile on Wasim's face, in which she sensed a moment of peacefulness. Yet the next second, he sank, thinking back about his fragmented family.

# Chapter 10

*Once I arrived in France, I underwent a lengthy and complex refugee status application process, which took two years to complete. The initial days weren't that pleasant. I had to live in worse conditions than I did all the way through here. I had regulations and restrictions. Identifying me as Syrian, the police had hassled for papers. After months of torment in the land that was supposed to offer safety, I was transferred to a better accommodation facility, where there were many unaccompanied minors like me. The government gave us education, yet I faced a range of challenges and obstacles in integrating into the new lifestyle.*

*I joined the American University of Paris a month after my eighteenth birthday. Of course, with financial aid and scholarships, I completed my education with graduation. And that is where I started evolving. I took advantage of the free language classes and learned French and English. I made myself proactive by benefiting from the extracurricular activities and grabbing all the internships and volunteer work opportunities. After having faced countless injuries and pain at a very young age, I decided to start playing some sport as that brings out both physical and emotional endurance. And it's from there that I'm continuing my passion for handball.*

"May I come in?" interrupted the doctor following a knock on the door. Riya, who was heavily engrossed in Wasim's life, collected herself and reconnected with the present reality.

The doctor entered to check Wasim's condition and assured him that he was improving. He also permitted Wasim to get discharged that evening on condition that he would follow the instructions given for a complete recovery. Advising that Wasim may want to consider counselling or support groups to cope with the emotional aftermath, he gave a few contacts to benefit from if needed.

After getting the discharge summary from the doctor, Riya put his file in her bag and helped him get off the bed.

"Let's go to my place," said Riya.

"No, no. That won't be right," Wasim was alarmed.

"Duh! It's my home. I live with my parents. We are not going to stay alone. Is that okay now?"

"No, it's not. I have my home. Okay, not a home, but a place of my own to live. I'll go there and take care of myself."

"You are still recovering, Wasim. You need someone to help."

"I don't live depending on anyone. I can…"

"I'm going to the reception to pay the bills. Is this the card that you use?" Riya interrupted in between, stretching out a bank card she had taken from his wallet.

"Yes, but give it to me. I'll pay and…"

"Okay, I'll be at the reception. Join me soon," she interrupted again and left the room, taking his card.

"What kind of girl is she? Why is she this keen to help me? This shouldn't be anything serious. I'm not in a place to handle all this craziness," Wasim thought to himself and started walking slowly towards the reception.

"Here's your card," Riya handed over it to Wasim after paying the bill. She then held his hand and started walking towards the exit door.

Wasim gently removed his hand from her grip to show he wasn't interested. Though Riya noticed it, she acted as if it didn't matter. As they got into the Uber, Wasim looked at Riya in an effort to scan what was inside her mind. Riya looked back at him. Their eyes met, and stared at each other.

Wasim seemed not to unlock this stare, so Riya quickly talked, "I apologise if you feel that I'm crossing my limits, commanding and overlooking your feelings. You can count me as your friend, and I would be happy to help you in this situation. This is not out of pity or to make you feel dependent on someone. I do not know in what regard you shared the most sensitive episodes of your life with me. But, knowing how much you have encountered, I believe that it's my duty to support you and be a part of finding your family. Yet again, I'm not pressing you to do this. Now, I'll let you choose for yourself. If you don't want to come with me, I'll drop you in your place," and smiled.

Wasim remained silent.

Riya continued, "Silence always doesn't mean a 'yes.' Sometimes, it says that one's tired of explaining. What does your silence mean?"

"Silence speaks when words can't. I have no words for an answer for you. Who are you? Why do you do all this to me? It's been so long since someone cared for me. This seems like an all-new feeling. I fear I would start liking it."

Silence embraced both as the driver stopped the car in front of Riya's apartment.

"This is my place. What have you decided?" asked Riya

Wasim exited the car and waited for Riya to get down and join him. Riya's joy knew no bounds. She jumped out, paid for the ride and led Wasim inside to her home. As he entered the hallway, he sensed a feeling of pleasantness and warmth. The entire house was harmonious, be it the unrivalled comfort of the carpet flooring, the fine modern furniture or the nice wall colours. He sat on the cushioned couch in the bright living room, looking at the sheer curtains swaying. He just loved the place.

Riya's mother came in and welcomed Wasim. After having a quick chat and expressing concern about his health, she informed him that Riya's father was on the way from his office and would be there soon. Wasim fixed his eyes on Riya's mother as she went inside the kitchen to bring him some refreshments.

"Do you like it here?" Riya wondered aloud.

"Yes, now I realise how living in a dreary 25m$^2$ studio apartment has made my life downcast," he spoke in response.

"Maybe it's time to change," Riya winked.

"Maybe it's not about the house," said Wasim.

Riya was sure about what he would say, yet she gave him an 'I'm ready to listen' look, and he continued, "This place is filled with love, comfort, a sense of belonging and purpose. You have a family to hold and lean on each other. That makes this beautiful house a home. I miss my family so much now."

Riya saw Wasim sinking into the bitter remembrance and had to act quickly to draw him out of it. She bounced in front of him and said, "Let me take you around the house. Come with me."

As Wasim joined her, she showed him around, talking so much without pausing so that he wouldn't have time to think about his bitter past. Wasim on the other hand, recognized Riya's efforts in trying to turn his distressing thoughts away and felt comfortable about it.

"This is a cosy nook where I curl up with a good book or a movie and a cup of coffee, sometimes a plate of Vadas and Badjis," she said, licking her lips.

"Plate of what?" asked Wasim with an enquiring glance. "Vadas and Badjis. Those are Indian snacks. As the French have 'le gouter' when one eats crepes and cookies, we have 'tea-time' to eat these in the evening, usually with a glass of tea. Would you like to taste them? I will ask my mother to make it for you," said Riya in an electrified tone.

Wasim smiled at her excitement for food and replied, "Sure. But some other day."

Riya then started speaking about her love for food. How she has a favourite spot in her hometown to eat parathas and how she travelled six hours, all the way from Kanchipuram to Karaikal to eat Mandi, while Wasim chimed in commenting, "Mandi is a Yemeni food. Do you get to eat that in India?"

As they were speaking, they reached Riya's room. Riya showed her room around and proposed to Wasim to have some rest. Wasim, who was not only tired but also diffident, instantly agreed and had a good repose in Riya's room. Hours later, Riya entered the room with a tray of filled-up bowls and plates.

"Here comes your dinner. Are you okay in here?"

"Ohh...thank you so much. But, have you all had your dinner?"

"Not yet. Dad's on a phone call. Mom and I will eat together with him once he finishes it. Now, let me help you with this."

Riya placed the tray carefully on the bedside table and was about to start serving when Wasim grasped her hand to stop. The coolness in his hand pierced through her skin and toured in all directions on the way to her heart. Her eyelids fluttered in jitters, and her cheeks blushed. She enjoyed the feel of his touch covertly and placed her warm hands on his and faced him.

"Are you cold? Shall I turn on the heater?"

"No, I'm fine. If you don't mind, may I join you for dinner?" "Sure, why not? I'm sorry, I should have asked you to join us, but it seemed to me that you might find it inconvenient. Okay, I'll keep all these on the dining table, and you can join us in ten minutes."

Before leaving the room, she turned back and said, "We would love to have you with us," and cast the loveliest smile at him that melted his heart.

* * *

At the dining table, Riya's father acquainted himself with Wasim while they were served hot fluffy parathas with chicken curry and some sauteed vegetable salad. Being of Middle Eastern origin, eating the parathas using his hand was not difficult for him. However, he was not habituated to spicy food. Seeing him not being able to eat it spicy, Riya rushed inside the kitchen to bring some yoghurt and served it on his plate.

"Try eating with this. Yoghurt will reduce the hotness of the curry. Else shall I make something less spicy for you?" asked Riya, expressing her concern.

Riya's mother and father looked at each other, observing Riya's attitude towards Wasim and sensed something anew in it.

"No, no. It's better now," responded Wasim, looking at Riya, who had already shifted her sight to her mobile. Though she didn't notice him, he continued looking at her after taking each bite of the paratha. Finally, when Riya realised she was being stared at with an intense gaze, her eyes refused to look straight into Wasim's eyes.

But not being able to wait anymore, Wasim called out aloud, "Riya, is this what you said 'parathas'?"

"Yes, yes. Riya's favourite," responded Riya's mother.

"The curry is so delicious, Amma," Wasim complimented, looking at Riya's mother.

Everyone exclaimed, "Amma!"

"Am I wrong? I heard Riya saying that word to her mother," Wasim was embarrassed.

Riya's father laughed and eased him, saying, "Amma is a beautiful word that means 'mother' in Tamil. We were just stunned to hear it from you."

Wasim's eyes welled up as he started to speak, "It's been nearly ten years since I last said this word. I can still recall how we were together at the dining table, the same as now before our hard time started. And then a lot happened. A lot." He exhaled heavily, breathing out all the pressure and looked at everyone, saying, "Riya's 'amma' is like 'ummi' to me."

Riya's father got up from his chair and ran to Wasim to give him the warmest hug he had ever had.

"Riya calls me 'dada,' and how do you call your father?" he asked.

"Baba," said Wasim.

Till midnight, the house was filled with both laughter and tears as they were all chatting. Riya's father looked at the clock and jumped out of the chair, crying, "It's 11:45 already. I have an important meeting tomorrow in Luxembourg. I need to be at the airport before 7:30. I'll take leave. You all continue if you want to."

"I'll help you pack your things. Come, let's go" said Riya's mother, and they both left.

"Wasim, you go and get some rest," said Riya as she removed the food platters from the table and entered the kitchen. She placed them into the sink and turned to see Wasim standing closely behind her, holding the bowls.

This time, there was a transformation in Wasim's eyes when compared to the last time at the stadium. The eyes filled with longing and loneliness changed to brighter and more focused. Riya intuited some kind of connection and passion in Wasim's eyes that was mirroring the deep emotions that were building up inside, with warmth and intensity. Looking at him this close stirred the reminiscence of how she wanted to see him, back in the stadium ground.

Coming out of the thoughts, she realised how deeply they were looking into each other's eyes. Her eyes shouted out how much she loved him and desired for him to grasp it. She wished he would drop the bowls and hug her so tight that she could transpierce through and get to the bottom of his heart. This thought made her close her eyes and turn her head to the side in desperation, and Wasim took a few steps backwards.

Riya cleared her throat and said, "Why do you have to do all this? I'll take care of it. You please get some rest for yourself."

Wasim replied, "I've never been this happy in so many days. Thanks to you. After all these years, I had dinner with a family at a dining table. Let me be fully satisfied by helping you with these chores like I used to do for my mother."

"OK then. But bring them one by one and be careful. You might hurt the wound in your hand," said Riya.

"Sure. I'll take care," he smiled.

* * *

A day later, Riya was getting ready.

"Maaaa…where is my blue dress that we bought for the wedding?" she shouted.

"It must be in your wardrobe. Look for it on the topmost shelf," said her mother.

"May I come? I'm sorry I'll be troubling you for a few minutes," Riya said to Wasim as she entered her room.

"Where are you going?" asked Wasim looking at her, who was running here and there in haste.

"Valerie, one of my colleagues is getting married. I need to … ah here it is!" she pulled out a beautiful dress and placed it on her shoulders with both hands. The dress cascaded and dangled over her. Standing in front of the mirror, she looked at how beautiful the dress was. Seconds later, she realised Wasim was looking at her from behind. Looking at him through the mirror without turning back, she asked, "How's it?"

"Nice, but…"

"But what?"

"It's nothing extraordinary. If I may say…"

"Of course, you may."

"Do you have something like what you wore that day when you came to the stadium to meet me?"

"Do you mean salwar kameez?"

"Salwar kameez, yes. How about wearing one?"

"But it's an Indian outfit."

"It does not matter. Would you mind trying once?"

"But…what if it doesn't work out? I'll be late."

"You'd look pretty in it," his eyes sparkled, admiring Riya.

Riya was slightly irked, yet she enjoyed realising how Wasim was thoughtful and showed interest in her. It also struck her that he had noticed what she wore that day and remembered it still. She ran to get dressed, like how Wasim wished to see her.

After about twenty minutes, she came wearing a breezy off- white flowy cotton frock-like kurta paired with white ankle-length palazzo pants. A tinge of indigo-blue printed dupatta pulled the outfit together. Her long, flowing, wavy tresses were pulled back into an elegant ponytail. Twisted rope-like braids on both sides from near her temple, pinned back and intertwined into the rest of her hair, would definitely make everyone stop and stare. She accessorised with a set of plain silver metal bangles on her right hand and a classic minimalist watch on her left hand.

Riya looked celestial in Wasim's eyes. He noticed everything that made her look attractive, and when she asked about what he thought of her outfit, he could only reply, "Gorgeous," unable to take his eyes off her.

Once she left, Wasim couldn't stop thinking about Riya and got down to contemplate the feelings he had started developing for her. The way she is concerned about him kindled his psyche. His unsettled mind thought of how she looked at him every time with passion and how she had constantly looked out for his well-being. He also realised how vulnerable and, at the same time, comfortable he was with her. He noticed himself falling for her.

# Chapter 11

The next morning, Riya walked from the kitchen to her nook with a mug of coffee. Wasim saw her crossing and came out of the room.

"Good morning," he said.

"Good morning, Wasim. Wait, I'll bring you coffee."

"No, no. It's ok. You first have yours. I'll make my coffee."

"Okay then. I'll go with you in case you need my help," she said teasingly.

"I'll just need help in locating things. Apart from that, I'm a pro cook," replied Wasim, winking at her.

Riya jumped and sat on the kitchen counter. Sipping her coffee, she assisted him. Wasim sensed it was the right time to inform her that he was leaving.

"Where are Mom and Dad?" he asked to initiate the conversation.

"They have gone to the airport to greet their friend from India."

"Okay. Riya, I'm leaving today."

She kept her half-empty coffee mug down, "Today! Why do you have to? …I mean…, why so early?"

"No, it's already too late."

"Too late for what? You were right in the middle of something terrible and have gone through a trauma. Your company has given you a month's leave, and your health …"

"It's neither about my health nor my work," Wasim burst out. "It's about you. The first time you came to meet me was to know why I looked at you as if I knew you. Okay, reasonable. But why did you come to the hospital after the attack? When I had no one in my life, why did you reassure me with your presence? Why did you bring me here and roped me into this beautiful family?" he broke down.

"Because I love you," she retorted, dissolving into tears.

Breaking the terrible silence, she continued, "The first time I came to meet you might seem logical to you, but it was not. It was not logical. In such a big stadium, in the middle of a massive crowd, why would you look at me? And why would I look at you? Thinking of it as a coincidence, I could have put it off. But I came to see you with the stupidest excuse. After the mosque attack, knowing that something grave had happened to you, I couldn't sit and watch you on TV. Then, in the hospital, when you told me about your life, I desired strongly to give you the love that you had missed for years."

Wasim spoke calmly, "I am not someone you think I am. I am not normal. I may look young, but I feel old. I feel old from all the misery I've seen. I can't be happy with you. I have been feeling dead for so many years. Life with someone like me is not going to be pleasurable. This could not be how you expect it to be"

"You were happy around me, and you realised it. That is the reason you want to leave now. You are scared. What I can't understand is, what are you scared of? For some reason, you don't want yourself to be happy. You willingly hold back the pleasures of your life."

"Enough," he roared again, "We both live in two different worlds, Riya. You can't understand. Better try to accept it."

Wasim left the coffee mug without having even a sip. He went inside the room to pick up his mobile phone and jacket. Riya was still sitting on the kitchen counter having a preoccupied look processing what had just happened.

Wasim came near the kitchen entrance, "Thank you very much for everything you've done for me. It is the least I can say to you," and left.

Once he left, "I am not the girl who cries and grieves and laments over someone," said Riya to herself, grabbing her bag and phone as she walked out of her home. She walked, walked, and walked until she could raise her head up and look at the tower, the Eiffel Tower. Every time she sees the towering structure, her eyes widen, and her finger traces its outline in the air. It never fails to amaze her. She has a spot on the left bank of the River Seine where she sits and enjoys the view of the tower. That is the place of both her bliss and her blues.

Seated on a stone bench, she gazed upon the doves alongside the river, walking, hopping, and flying. She thought to herself, "I was as free as these birds. Now, I pushed myself into a cage, a cage that the owner never wanted to visit. I was independent, and now I don't know why my happiness depends on him. I have given that much power over my life to him. It's been only days, yet I feel I have known him for years, and I miss him. Where would I search for him again? Even if I know where to go, what will I do there?"

Her lips quivered as she reflected on her love for him, and tears fell on her hands drop by drop. She tried to resist crying, but mulling over the fact that Wasim had rejected her pushed her down in the dumps and made her burst into tears. She came to the tower hoping it would heal her, but this time, it failed. Because the damage this time was intense and profound. Quickly, Riya wiped her face and started walking in an attempt to distract herself. She strolled randomly until she reached a juncture. On her way there, she had already broken down a hundred times thinking of him. She couldn't handle it anymore, so she took a bus back home.

"Where is Wasim?" asked her father.

"He left" replied Riya.

"Where?" her father asked again.

"To his home? Where else?" she countered in an annoyed tone.

"But there isn't anyone to take care of him!" worried her mother.

"A lone wolf he is. He doesn't need anyone, nor do we need him," She flared up and went into her room.

As she shut the door and sat against it, the smell of Wasim still lingering in her room slowly flowed in the air, waiting for her to breathe it in. Once she drew it in, all the beautiful memories with him flooded before her. She fiercely opened the windows and lit her room with tens of scented candles, trying to fade his smell out. Riya, who became physically and mentally exhausted, fell into her bed to again feel the presence of Wasim in it. But this time, she didn't want to get rid of it. Lying on her side, she amassed the blanket to bury her face inside and slept crying.

A little later, her mother, who sensed something was not right with her, came inside, bringing lunch for her. She shut all the windows, turned off the candles, and sat near Riya on her messy bed. Stroking on her hair, she woke her up.

"Wake up. I'll feed you."

"No, Mom. I'm not hungry."

"I know you won't be hungry. But it would be better if you had something. I've made your favourite chicken fried rice. Come on. Get up, baby."

Riya got up with tears running down her cheeks and hugged her mother.

"It's difficult for me to bear this pain," said Riya, getting the plate from her mother and started eating.

"Darling, you've been brought up inside a shell. Thus far, we have protected you from facing any heartbreak. Now, this pain and suffering is the breaking of the shell. You've grown out of the shell; there is way more to go. It's time for us to stop keeping you from harm and you to learn how to overcome this. But darling, never forget that we are forever there to guide you and back you. Now, tell me, what's the problem?"

"Mom, I like Wasim so much. He likes me too, and he could see how much I love him. But he is still stuck in his past and not ready to come out of it, no matter how his life has been bettered"

"Hmm…how long have you known him, Riya?"

"Mom, that's not the issue…"

"How long do you know him?" Riya's mother interrupted and asked again.

"A week," replied Riya dismally.

"Do you think you had given him enough time to understand you and you to understand him?"

Riya sighed.

Her mother continued, "Wasim's life's not like yours, both in the past and present."

"This is what he says too."

"Because that is the truth. He's gone through a lot which you can never imagine. Give him time. Let him realise by himself how important you are going to be in his life. Let him realise you are capable of changing his life. Let him realise that you give a new purpose for him to live. Wait for it."

Riya ate the food without talking about anything more. After her mother left, she noticed Wasim's hospital file on the table. She found his house address in it and considered going there to give the file and meet him. But, as her mother said, she decided to give him some time and wait.

* * *

A few days later, she had to go to the prefecture for a conference. While she entered through the personnel and staff gate, she noticed a group of people trying to enter without an appointment via the public gate. She asked the security guard about it, and he explained that they were asylum seekers, instantly reminding her of Wasim. At that moment, she felt the difference Wasim mentioned.

"If we come to this place together, I would have good memories that make me feel delighted about my successful career. But he would grieve over the unpleasant memories. While he suffers, how could I share my happiness? And while I want to share my joy with him, how will he overcome his grieving? This is indeed complicated," she reflected silently.

As she entered, she noticed a young Arabian boy with his grandmother trying hard to make the security guard understand what they wanted. He spoke Arabic, however, stressing the few English words he knew. The guard, who doesn't speak English, was not able to grasp even the few words the boy said. Looking at them struggling with each other, Riya swiftly reached them.

"Hello. May I help you?" she said in English as the three stared at her. She looked at the guard and repeated in French, "Puis-je vous aider?"

He asked her back, "Parlez-vous arabe?" (Do you speak Arabic?) Riya took her phone from her pocket and said, "Non, mais je peux vous aider," (No, but I can help you) as she opened the Translate app.

She typed: "Tell me how I may help you?" and tapped the play icon. She quickly stretched her phone out to the boy as the voice translated it into Arabic. The boy slowly smiled approvingly and started speaking out in Arabic to the phone. Following this trivial help, she made a big decision to take Arabic classes with the intention of helping the Arab migrants, which would also be advantageous for her career. But deep inside, she perceived that it was for Wasim. The thought of being able to communicate with Wasim in his native language filled her with a sense of joy and purpose.

* * *

The following day, she took Wasim's file and left for his house. In Pantain, one of the suburbs of Paris, he was living in a small studio apartment near a busy commercial centre. Standing in front of the main entrance door, Riya searched for Wasim's name in the external panel of the intercom system. Figuring it out, she reached for the corresponding button to ring the bell, thinking about what she would say when he answered the call.

But before she could ring, she heard someone from behind, "Whom do you want to meet, madam?"

She was startled hearing the voice and turned towards him. Though Wasim was initially shocked to see her there, there was also some kind of happiness that he was trying to hide inside. Having him before his eyes, she wanted to let him know that she missed him badly, but she knew it wasn't the right time, so she pretended she was fine and replied, "I heard a wise man named Wasim lives here. I'm here to meet him" for which Wasim laughed and gestured for her to get in as he opened the door using the code.

They both were at a loss for words until they reached the fourth floor in the lift and got into Wasim's house. Once they were in, "How are you?" asked Wasim avoiding looking into her eyes.

"Great. And you?" responded Riya.

"I'm good. What would you like to have?"

"What are the choices you have for me?"

"Anything for you," he replied instinctively.

Riya, who was having a look around his house, suddenly turned towards him. Wasim tried to correct his words.

"I mean… anything you want–coffee, tea or juice."

"What's your special, Mr. Pro cook?"

"Cool. I'll make Ayran for you."

"Ayran? What's that?"

"It's a Middle Eastern traditional drink, very refreshing."

"I'm ready to try it," she said with her usual excitement for food.

She sat on the couch and looked at Wasim entering the open kitchen. She asked him, "How's your hand? Is it better now?"

Before he could reply, she was reminded about his hospital file. She took it out and kept it on the table. She also informed him about the file and told him that it was from that file that she found his address.

"If you'd known that I'd come searching for you with this file, you would've never forgotten and left it at my home," she said mockingly.

"What if I had willingly left the file there?" asked Wasim with a loving tone and passionate look.

"But why would you do that?" questioned Riya.

"Maybe I want you to come looking for me."

"And why is that?"

"Here's your drink," Wasim gave her a glass of Ayran.

After tasting it, Riya smacked her lips, saying, "Mmmm…this is yum. And it's much like the Indian buttermilk."

"Ohh, then this is not something new to you. Okay, will make Jallab for you another day."

"Does that mean you are inviting me here again?"

"Shouldn't I?"

"Will you?" she looked into his eyes.

Riya, not being able to look longer, tilted her head down. But Wasim couldn't stop looking at her with so much admiration. His eyes expressed how much he missed her in these few days. He realised how he laughed when she was around. He understood that her presence was the essence of his life. He took a look around his house and observed how, all at once, it became paradise. With a beaming smile, he again looked at her, sipping the drink from the glass. His mind oscillated between letting her know how much he missed her and not raising her hopes on something unsuitable for her. He swiftly changed to his long face and replied,

"Why am I going to call you again? Anyway, thank you for visiting and bringing the file. I was thinking of getting my hand checked with the doctor tomorrow."

Riya placed the empty glass on the table and stood up. She collected her things and sighed deeply.

"I have got the contact of a source who might help us find your family. Even if you don't want to accept my help, I'm going to do this for you. I'll let you know how things are regarding that. Do remember one thing, if you never heal from what hurt you, you'll bleed on people who try to heal you."

Riya left without turning back or taking leave from him. Wasim sank onto the couch after hearing this from her and seeing her leave. This time, it was Wasim who wanted to run behind her. Hold her hand to stop taking any steps further away from him.

He wanted to lift her up in his arms and take her back to his house. But all he did was let her go and stare at the way she just left.

# Chapter 12

It had been three days since Riya left Wasim, and her thoughts consumed his mind mightily. Thanks to Riya's Instagram public profile account. Wasim ran down on it and came to know that she was travelling to Geneva for an interview. He didn't want to spend a second, thinking if he should go. He rented a car and started to Geneva immediately.

Once reaching the city, he again checked her Instagram story for updates on where she was staying. Unfavourably, there were no stories and no posts. He parked the car in a rest area and waited a few more hours, a few more hours, and a few more. Sitting inside the car for a very long time fatigued him. He got out of the car, went to the washroom to relieve himself, and walked towards the nearest coffee shop while his phone beeped. It was an office mail from his office on which he was not ready to concentrate. Before putting his phone again into his jacket, he checked Riya's profile again for the nth time. Voila! This time, he saw a green ring circling her profile picture, showing she had updated something on her story.

He quickly clicked on her story to see what she had shared. As he scrolled through the images and videos, a smile slowly spread across his face, seeing a stunning photo of Riya dining at a restaurant. He typed the name of the tagged restaurant 'Thuy Hang' in Google Maps and brightly smiled as it was just a ten-minute drive from where he had been stationed. He immediately hastened to the restaurant and searched for a place to park his car. Due to lack of parking space, he circled the street twice, hoping a parking spot would open up. Before he could find one, he saw a group of four guys standing around a girl a few metres away from the restaurant entrance.

At first, it seemed like she was one among them, but Wasim felt something was not right. So, he parked the car and walked towards them. As he neared, he was shaken to see Riya being mocked and taunted by them. Wasim pounced with lightning speed to rapidly push two of them aside with his elbows and held Riya's hand. He could clearly see that they were blindly drunk, and it was not going to be challenging to collapse them. The other two raised their arms and almost pounced on him.

Riya hid herself behind Wasim, clutching his hoodie tight. Wasim simply put his leg forward and sidestepped. Phew! They both stumbled on each other and fell flat. The two, whom he jostled away first, closed in on him, his back firmly pressing against the cold stone wall. In the nick of time, before they could blow a strike on Wasim, he took one leg forward to position himself, opened both his palms and with utmost power, moved his right arm forward like an arrow, thrusting straight onto one of the drunkard's chin. The next second, his left palm attacked the other's nose.

Ensuring that all four had fainted, Wasim searched their pockets for their wallets and took those with him. He noticed Riya started walking and sat on a wooden park bench a few steps away. Wasim hastened to join her on the bench. Sitting next to her, he gathered his words, "Where do you stay? I'll drop you there."

"That's not your job," replied Riya coldly.

He breathed in a deep lungful of air and continued, "In the stadium, at first instinct, I thought you were the girl from the NGO, but seconds later, even when I realised you were not, I couldn't take my eyes off you. In our second meeting, at the stadium gate, I didn't want to part with you, and I stood there until you disappeared from my sight. But you never looked back. I believed this was definitely not going to work."

Riya, losing her grit, turned towards him, holding her tears. Wasim, who couldn't look into her eyes, got off the bench, took a few steps forward, and continued talking.

"When you came to the hospital, I wasn't in my senses. I desperately needed someone to share my grief and pain. Thankfully, it was you and I started falling for you. That's the reason I couldn't deny when you invited me home. Those were the best days since I was back in Syria with my family. I started enjoying living at your home. But, if I had expressed my love for you there, at your home, it would have meant that my love was for your family and home, not solely for you. Also, the differences between us and our lifestyles provoked guilt inside me. I didn't want to ruin your life. But when I saw you again at my place, I realised how much I missed you and to what extent you prevailed in my life. Sadly, I was not daring enough to tell you that. I was struggling inside to somehow let you know my feelings. And that is when you opened up about finding Aqeel. If I had expressed my love at that moment, it would have been sensed as a love out of gratitude, again not solely for you."

He turned back towards Riya.

"I wished that you comprehend my love for you is purely for you, not for anything else or anyone else. For this reason, to show you how important you are to me, I travelled all the way here."

Wasim kneeled in front of Riya, held both her hands, and continued, "This world had deceived me. But now, I can stand up and win it with my one hand, only if you hold my other for a lifetime."

The poor dim lights on the dark road suddenly glared brightly. A mild breeze gently caressed their faces and made the hairs sway. The floral fragrance of Linden trees all along the road, with added hints of honey and lemon, spread all over briskly. The ambience changed completely and gave them a taste of paradise.

Riya, who had already started letting her tears down, embraced him as she was sitting on the bench. As Wasim hugged her, lying his head on her lap, she bent and snuggled him.

"It's been so long since I had a lap to rest. I feel secure and soothed," said Wasim, looking up at Riya.

"From now on, it's upon me to give you the feeling of being safe and secure, to give you love and laughter, a tranquil heart, wings to your dreams, and joy forever after," replied Riya, cupping his face.

After a few minutes of exchanging fondness, they walked along the road holding hands until they reached the hotel where Riya stayed.

"Can you stay with me tonight? Tomorrow is an important day in my career. I have a job interview in the UN, and I'd love to have you with me," she perked up.

"Sure, but I will leave you here and go to my car tonight. Will join you early in the morning tomorrow."

"Have no fear. You can trust me," she laughed as she noticed Wasim blushing.

"Actually, It's in the parking lot. It would be better if I drive it here."

"I'll go with you."

Wasim left the wallets he took from the drunkard bullies' pockets in the post office and walked towards the parking. During this short trip, Riya discussed what happened in the prefecture that day.

*While leaving the conference hall, I saw the old lady, whom I helped translate to the security guard, sitting alone in the waiting hall. I approached her and tried to have a conversation, of course, using my mobile phone. I asked her about her grandson, and the answer she gave was pathetic.*

*"He is neither my son's son nor my daughter's son. God gives us family, and it's God who takes them back in the most ruthless manner. I had a son and a daughter, and they had children. In the war, I lost everyone. Three of them were killed, and a few were lost. I was left all*

*alone in the Zaatari refugee camp in Jordan. When we had lost the given family, we chose our family. He was my choice. We both chose each other. We have been living together for years, and I would like to forget that he is not my own flesh and blood."*

*Feeling dejected, I was about to leave when I heard the old lady calling the young boy. Hearing his name, I ran to them again. I stood facing the boy, breathing heavily and hoping he would reply affirmatively.*

*I asked him, "Are you Aqeel?"*

*Those few seconds, I couldn't handle the wait. My heart throbbed, and I was able to hear it outside.*

*"No," he replied, letting me down and abandoning all hopes. He continued, "I'm Adeel."*

*I settled myself into a chair, remembering everything about Aqeel from what you said. The boy sat next to me and signalled to take my phone. He spoke to it, and it conveyed:*

*"Thank you very much for your help back then. I think you are in distress now. It seems like you are searching for someone. There are many Aqeels in Syria, and I know an Aqeel back in the Zaatari refugee camp. If you would give more details about him, I can tell you if he is the one I know."*

*I spoke back to the phone, "He must be of your age, give or take a few years. And... yeah, his name is Aqeel. He has an elder brother. And...and..."*

*I murmured to myself, "Is that all I know about Aqeel? Didn't Wasim say something more? I couldn't bring anything from the back of my mind."*

*The boy, Adeel, replied, "Yes, he is two years older than me, but the brother of the Aqeel I knew is dead."*

*I was lost. I didn't know what to reply as I was unsure if that was your brother. Yet, I didn't want to pass over this information. So, I asked the boy to tell me whatever he knew about Aqeel and recorded it. I have sent it to a few of my friends who can help to find him in Jordan. Let's hold out hope."*

Riya played the recording to Wasim, and when he heard the boy describing, his eyebrows frowned, his nose turned red, and tears gushed out from those still eyes.

He closed his eyes tight and said, "This is my brother. The hazel eyes are from my mother, and the curly hair is my father's." He opened his eyes and continued, "That is how we lost him. I'm now excited to see how he would look as an adult now. Riya, you are reaching him. I guess we are not very far. You are my angel," he exclaimed and went about hugging her but curbed. Noticing this, Riya jumped on him and hugged him tight until he hugged her back. Riya's embrace comforted him as the weight of his emotions lifted.

"Jordan! I still wonder how I survived in a strange country, and now, I am being told about my little brother in an unknown country," Wasim mumbled in a hushed voice.

"By the way, do you have Aqeel's picture?" asked Riya

"No, I took my dad's phone when I left them. And lost it in the camp years back. All I have now are their faces imprinted in my heart."

"Oh la la. Then can I see them in your heart?" asked Riya playfully, leaning towards his chest.

Wasim stopped walking so as to have another cute moment with Riya. She laid her head on his chest, and he brought his arm around, holding her close.

"I can see your mother, father, a small boy, and…yeah, there is a girl. She is newly printed, and wait, she is beautiful…" she said and laughed.

Wasim laughed and embraced her.

* * *

In the hotel room, Wasim was waiting for Riya, who had been in the bathroom for a long time. As he was extremely tired after a long day, he gradually lounged on the cosy bed and into the blanket. When he heard the bathroom door open,

"How long? Are you okay?" he asked sleepily.

"Yes, I am. It's just my bedtime skincare routine," she responded as she noticed how tired Wasim looked. She offered him a relaxing face massage with her super refreshing exfoliator cream. But all he wanted was a good, peaceful sleep. He had already drifted off. So, Riya lay down on the other side of the bed, holding Wasim's hand and fell asleep.

# Chapter 13

After the interview, Riya and Wasim planned to drive to Chateau de Chillon, an island castle in Lake Geneva. It took them around an hour to get there. They parked the car in Montreaux, a nearby city, and set off walking to the castle along the lake. Strolling in the lovely weather for half an hour, they reached the castle. Though the fairytale-like castle had much to see inside it, they preferred watching the distant Alps and the surrounding turquoise water from outside.

"I had always wanted to tour Switzerland by car, to get off the roads and enjoy the scenery. But I never really thought my first trip here could be this beautiful. You made this trip beautiful, thank you," Riya expressed.

"Thank you. You are making my life beautiful," Wasim replied winking at her.

After spending good moments together, it was when they reached the car that Riya noticed her phone was missing. She repeatedly searched her handbag while Wasim saw her phone on the car dashboard ringing. They entered the car and found that her phone had been ringing non-stop for a long time. Riya checked on her phone and exclaimed,

"Oh, my! 21 missed calls from Alexandre! Hope everything is fine," she mumbled.

She then played the audio message he had sent her, "Riya, this is Alexandre. If you are still behind the boy, Aqeel, I beg you to stop it right away, do you understand? Stop searching for him. Call me when you are back without any delay."

Wasim and Riya looked at each other frightfully.

"What happened? What happened to Aqeel? Can you call him immediately and ask about it?" Wasim jittered.

Riya dialled Alexandre, who picked up the call in just one ring.

"What happened, Alex? What is it about Aqeel?" she gabbled.

"The boy has been accused of terrorism. Do you remember the Pantin mosque attack? The police grabbed him right at the spot, but he had managed to escape later. The police force is intensely tracking him down. I warn you again, stop looking for him," and he cut the call.

Riya placed her hand on Wasim's shoulder and shook him back to his senses.

"Wasim?"

"How is it even possible, Riya? I was the one who confronted the gunman. Couldn't I recognize my brother? Okay, he had his face covered. Was it not possible for him to identify me? He shot at me. He killed so many other people. That is definitely not Aqeel. By the way, why should a Muslim terrorist attack a mosque? It doesn't make sense. What happened to these people?"

"Wasim, something's not right. Let's try to sort it out. First,

let's go home. I'll drive the car."

All along the way, Wasim was lamenting and denying the accusation regarding his brother as Riya was comforting him. When they reached Paris, Riya decided to stay with Wasim, as he was not stable. That evening, they called Alexandre again to get more information on this.

"Is it anything about that boy?" Alex questioned.

"Alex, please listen to me patiently. This has to be a mistake or misunderstanding or whatever. How did you get to know about this?" Riya asked back.

"Okay, you asked me to enquire about a boy named Aqeel in the Zataari camp, didn't you?"

"Yes, I did."

"My girlfriend has one of her friends working in the Office of Research, UNICEF, Italy. She reached the data and learnt that Aqeel had been in the camp for four years. Then, he had been transferred to two other camps in the next four years, after which he had gone missing from the records. Some people living in the camp since then have given information. They have said that the boy Aqeel has been lured into one of the militant organisations fighting against the Syrian government, whose name I don't want to mention. Meanwhile, that particular organisation gave a video announcement claiming the mosque attack employing their member named Aqeel."

"But this is absurd. Why should a Muslim organisation attack a mosque?"

"I don't understand the logic, nor do I want to."

"Thank you, Alex. Good night."

"I'm sorry, Riya, I couldn't help you more on this."

"What you have done now is a big thing. Thank you very much."

* * *

Riya ordered dinner for them. After having the sandwiches, Riya couldn't sleep, but she made Wasim sleep on her lap. She began to contemplate everything from the beginning and asked herself,

"Generally, while these organisations take claim of an attack, they don't mention the individual's name. But why did they do it in Aqeel's case? Is it because he had already been caught, and the police would have gathered all his information? Or do they want to deliberately use his name? Or could there be any other reason? To know what actually happened, we need Aqeel. Maybe he is a criminal, maybe not, but surely, he must be in hiding now. How do we bring him to us? Perhaps if he sees his brother and knows that he is still searching for him."

Wasim suddenly woke up from a nightmare, shouting, "I see blood everywhere. I feel blood. He's running. Someone take off his mask."

Riya relieved him from it and gave him some water to drink. Once he came to his senses, he said to Riya, "Riya, I loved my country, but my country abandoned us. This country embraced me as its citizen, and I am living a decent and peaceful life here. This is the time to show my gratitude. If it is Aqeel, there is zero chance that I'll try to protect him."

She hugged him tight and laid her head on his chest.

"I can hear your heart say something contrary," she said.

"Yes, because I'm certain it is not Aqeel," he replied.

"Are you certain because he's your brother?"

"No, because Aqeel is left-handed."

Riya sprang from the couch in excitement.

"Aqeel is in danger. We must meet him so that we can help him," said Riya.

"It is more difficult to search for him now than before," Wasim grieved.

"It is. But I have a plan. Luckily, we don't have to search for him in Syria or Jordan. He must be somewhere in or around Paris. We need to let him know that you are his brother and you are still waiting for him. This would make him come out of his hiding spot to meet you. And for that, how about you giving an interview on TV channels? If luck favours us, Aqeel could see you and try to reach you."

"This is, in fact, a good idea, but I am not comfortable with…"

"Even not for your brother?"

"Okay, I'll do it," he reluctantly agreed, realising that this was the best chance to help his long-lost brother from the trap.

* * *

Riya made arrangements with a few TV channels and YouTube channels to interview Wasim, presenting him as the Pantin mosque attack survivor. Talking about the shooting attack, he deviated to talk about his life in Syria.

"You live in a country where you are safe. You have a government to protect you. You have freedom. You do what you want to. You're free to support whomever you want. You live without any restrictions. You are very fortunate. You merrily cuddle with your loved ones inside your home. You don't have to worry about your children's lives.

But there is a country in the Middle East, in the middle of the world map. You can call it the land of curse. There, we constantly have the fear of losing our loved ones. Since the war, as many as 25,000 children have been killed and many more lost. Among them was my then-8-year-old brother. We lost him years ago and are still unable to locate him.

While many of our women are subjected to unspeakable atrocities involving sexual assaults, forced abortions, and torture, men are forcefully recruited for combat and get killed or injured as combatants. In Syria, it is mass murder upon mass murder, atrocity upon atrocity. To be a Syrian entangled in this conflict is to be cut off from every law and principle.

We flee war, oppression, tyranny, and economic downturn. We know war as good as you know peace. There is fighting in our country, fighting with deadly weapons. We are shot with rifles. Our homes are destroyed with missiles. Anyone who could get away from the bloodshed must do that. We can't sit tight and wait to be killed. No one risks the lives of our family and children in such a way except out of utter desperation. We seek refuge in other countries and yet we see news every day anticipating for the war to stop.

When the hostility stops there, we will stop coming here as refugees and will go back. We need governments to help us. It is not still a lack of information. It is a lack of political willingness which is a step closer to peace. It must be much easier for you to do that than for us to go back and live amidst the warfare. If you experience what it is like there, you'll support us.

The large majority of Syrians who decide to flee Syria take shelter and stay in camps along the Syrian border in Turkey, Lebanon or Jordan at the outset. Some travel west, through Turkey, arriving at coastal cities such as Izmir. After arriving there, thousands of refugees stay in tents on the Aegean coast of Turkey preparing their way across the eastern Mediterranean to Greece by boat. Although they are aware, they prefer to be preyed upon by criminal gangs along the coastline who apparently charge a fortune to transport them to Greece.

Some travel to Egypt and take the trans-Mediterranean route there. All these routes are dangerous and uncertain as we cross the Mediterranean often in insubstantial boats, which are in a position to make even the brief ride from Turkey to Greece threatening. But they don't want to miss any possibility that would take them to safety, even if it is facing a dangerous journey in adverse weather across the Aegean Sea in loaded rubber dinghies. According to UNHCR, an estimated 20,000 people have died or gone missing so far while attempting to cross the Mediterranean Sea.

The fear of travelling by sea makes the Balkan route, the only other option, the most relied upon to enter the EU. Even when you get through the land, you're not safe as you risk death, capture and deportation. It's hard all the way through. We are famished, cold, intimidated and yet can't do anything. Usually, we are crammed into trucks and tankers, risking suffocation to death. There are instances where people die slowly and painfully due to lack of oxygen in an enclosed space and difficulty breathing as they had been crammed into trucks. Our country has pushed us out, and we are being treated as goods.

But even once in the EU, we have to stand up to the European countries doing all they can to keep us out. Greece has built a border and denies the reports of pushback. Hungary has closed its border, forcing refugees to travel west through Croatia. Even when we never felt protected, even when we never felt welcomed, even with all the brutality from the border control and police, even with the mud and the cold and the hunger and the unsanitary circumstances, it's better here than in our homeland.

Countries spend millions on building high razor-wire fences along the border, setting up thousands of guards, and sending the army to prevent us from entering and crossing over. They deploy water cannons and tear gas on the refugees at the border. Yet they are disinclined to spend money on helping us.

All that we ask is a mere peaceful life with the bare necessities. We don't live in houses. We live under tarpaulin tents. We have very few toilets and a few standpipes for hundreds of us. Without drainage, the camp becomes a muddy pool when it rains. Voluntary medical caregivers affirm that hundreds of fresh injuries are treated in the camp on a daily basis. Overcrowded and cold conditions lead to the treatment of scabies and other respiratory diseases.

Legal and recognised camps get provisions, shelter and food from government groups and other non-governmental organisations. However, this is not the case in many other camps that are not recognized. The non-governmental organisations couldn't support them, fearing they would lose their funding from the government. Yet some of them endeavour to make the government effectuate the basic needs for us despite the slashing of the right-wing group at them. So inevitably, we become principally dependent on charity from the public, through unofficial charitable groups.

If we could work and earn our living, we would bring our bread to our tables. But we aren't permitted to work. We have no jobs as we are called illegal migrants. We scrupulously spend the savings we brought along. Again, those who don't have any savings wholly rely on donations.

Furthermore, animosity against us increases, violence frequents, we are harassed, we are abused, we are beaten, and we are bitten by dogs. I am not talking about those who work with care, concern, and conscientiousness to protect the rights and safety of refugees and asylum seekers because I was one of those who rebuilt their lives with the help of people like them. Thanks to the respective bodies that enforce accountability and hold the police accountable for their actions, in my case.

We are already dealing with deleting the bad memories of abandoning our beautiful homes and our desperate country. We just ask you not to give us more miserable memories to delete.

We still hope for a new beginning, a new future, and possibly the end of the war in Syria. That's all we want. Do you still think it's too much for us to ask?"

# Chapter 14

$A$ week later, Riya received an email asking her to join the training after successfully being selected in the UN interview. She was equally both happy and down seeing the mail. She went to Wasim, who was doing the dishes and hugged him from behind.

"What happened, Ri?"

"Ri? That's how my mom calls when she is in a great mood."

"Yes, I took note of that. Okay, tell me now. What happened?"

"I have been called for the training to Geneva."

"That means you got selected! Felicitation, mon cherie."

"The training is for one year."

"Don't you want to go?"

"I do, but I don't want to leave you either."

Wasim loosened Riya's grip from his waist and turned towards her. She, who didn't want to show her crying face to him, at once covered her face with his t-shirt, resting her head on his chest.

"Riya, isn't this your dream? I'm happy that I'm with you at this moment. Dreams coming true moment is not for everyone. We are fortunate. I'm not going anywhere. I'll forever wait here for you. But this opportunity in your career won't wait. By the way, my emergency medical leave is just about to end, and I'll start going to work this Monday. So, let's do this together," comforted Wasim.

"You don't love me enough. That is why you don't feel bad," said Riya fussily.

"This is something new to you, Riya, but not for me. I have sustained the pain of separation and…"

"Can't you say you feel bad, at least for my sake?" she fussed again.

"Okay, I feel bad, and I'll miss you, Riya."

"Ri," she corrected, still burying her face into him.

"Yes, Ri. I'll miss you, Ri. I'll miss you terribly," he said, as he held her shoulders and parted her from him. He pecked delicately on her forehead.

"What will you do when you miss me?" asked Riya, caressing his neck with her fingers.

"I'll call you," replied Wasim, placing his hands on her waist and pulling her closer.

"If I don't pick up?" her hands wrapping around his neck and feet stretching up.

"I… I'll," Wasim couldn't speak looking at her this close. He tried hard to come out of her deep eyes and fell again for her lips.

Their hearts accelerated as they forgot the world around them for the moment. Their breaths and bodies fused together as a single entity, letting their lips run into each other and kissing passionately. As they explored each other deeply, Wasim realised Riya had frozen, and he slowly retreated, still letting his lips linger on hers until she pulled away with a shaking exhale and dropped her forehead into his neck coyly.

He held her gently, feeling the tremors in her body, and whispered softly, "Are you okay?"

Riya nodded, her voice barely a whisper as she replied, "I'm just overwhelmed…in the best way possible."

* * *

That weekend, Riya prepared herself for her one-year stay in Geneva and spent time at her home with her parents and Wasim together. On Sunday afternoon, Wasim proposed to drive her to Geneva. On the way, he checked on everything, like the apartment where she would stay, food, her daily transportation plan, and the travel passes. Riya had everything settled already and was factoring in what to do if Aqeel wanted to contact his brother. She was considering places to meet him and other ways to communicate without being tracked. She alerted Wasim to always be aware of what was happening around him.

"If you sense something unusual or feel some random person is trying to get in contact, it could be Aqeel. If he reached us and we succeed in proving that the gunman is right-handed and Aqeel is left-handed, it's done. You being one of the victims of the attack is an advantage as you are an eyewitness. At the same time, be careful. We still don't know what exactly is happening around us. There could be potential dangers."

"Calm down, Riya. I will manage. I never imagined I could put up through all the rough times and make it here. Now, I'm psyched up to do this again for my brother."

"My long-held dream is turning into reality now. But your pain of many years is not very far from finding its medicine, and at this very moment, I couldn't be with you," she complained.

"Riya, I strongly feel that God has chosen you to meet me because you are the one who is going to bring my family to me. If not now, whenever that miracle happens it's going to be because of you. So, don't worry. Until then, I'll take care."

* * *

Dropping her at her apartment, Wasim returned to Paris and rejoined his work. Back in Geneva, the first week was extremely industrious, and Riya had time only to bustle between the workload and settling down stuff. Though she didn't get time to call Wasim, she constantly thought of him. Sometimes, while handling work stress, homesickness, and the absence of Wasim, she held back her tears by singing songs aloud and not letting anyone know what was happening in her life. On the other side, Wasim called her twice and received a message that she was busy and would call later. So, he didn't want to distract her from focusing on her dream and waited for her to call back.

* * *

After a week, she called Wasim. Wasim grabbed his phone in great joy, looking at Riya's name on it.

"Come here immediately," she ordered.

"What happened, Riya? Are you okay?" he asked panic-stricken.

"I'm okay, Wasim. Can you please come here immediately? I mean, start right now. I think I am seeing Aqeel right in front of me."

"Aqeel? But, he…how?"

"Wasim! Quick."

"I'm starting."

Wasim left his office and ran to the train station. After having bought the ticket and settled down in a seat, he called Riya. She didn't pick up but messaged him back.

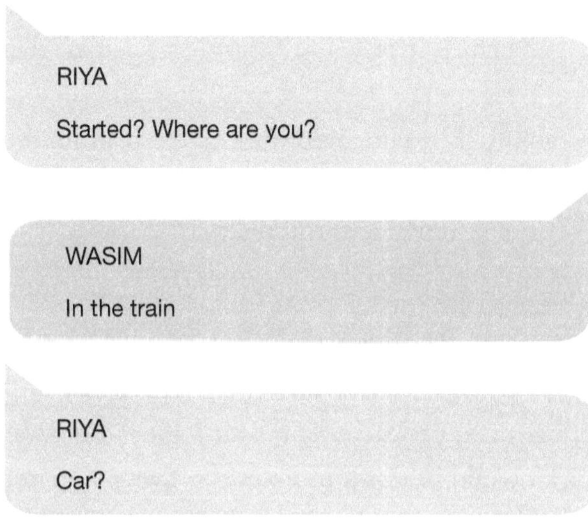

> **WASIM**
>
> No, not in the state to drive
>
> This takes less time than that
>
> Will reach before 3 pm

> **RIYA**
>
> Great
>
> I can't call right now Call me once you reach here. In case, I can't pick up the call, I'll send you my location. Come here straight away.

That three-hour journey reminded Wasim of his boat journey from Croatia to Italy. The waves daunted the whole of them by pushing up and pulling down. At each wave, their heartbeats skipped, and before they could return to normal, there came another wave. He couldn't help but recall the feeling of uncertainty and vulnerability he experienced during that boat journey. Same as that, this entire journey shook him down with turbulent emotions that consumed him throughout.

"My darling boy Aqeel! Is it really him? If yes, what is he doing there? How could Riya have identified him? Maybe she would have talked with him. Or is it just a guess of hers? By the way, the French police must be searching for him. How did Riya see him in public? How did he go from France to Swiss? Could he really be the one who attacked the mosque? Let me ask him directly.

What if he says yes?" Wasim's heart throbbed faster with the last question.

"Okay, I can't deal with this for long. Whatever it is, I'll face it once I reach there and see him face-to-face. Now, let me think about something pleasant," he said to himself and closed his eyes to recollect the memories of how he reacted when he saw Aqeel as a newborn in the hospital, how he used to recite him stories at night, how they both went to school together and played in their backyard in their beautiful home in Syria. These thoughts enraged him more. His mind unintentionally started thinking about the present again, then the past, and then the future. His weary brain fell asleep, and the train had already halted at Geneva when he woke up.

* * *

"Mr. President, foreign ministers, your excellencies, ladies and gentlemen, it's an honour to brief the council. I thank the High Commissioner for Refugees, the members of Hand in Hand for Syria, my benefactors who aided me all the way here, and the Global Refugee Forum for this opportunity.

Any refugee can speak eloquently about this deepening humanitarian calamity as I do now, for the reason that these are words from our experiences that give us this strength and resilience. Over 20 million Syrians, it's really a big number, have been victimized by a conflict we have no part in. Yet, we are traumatized and stigmatized. So, I, Aqeel from Syria, am here to represent our people in this United Nations, our United Nations. We have been displaced from our homeland and considered a burden in all other countries. I question, if this United Nations was a country of its own, would it have taken us into safety?

The purpose of the UN is to maintain peace and security, bring countries together, prevent and end conflicts, find diplomatic solutions, and save lives. But all crimes that the Humanitarian Law prohibits happen every day in Syria. Nevertheless, the Security Council's power to address these threats lies unused, failing to save us from those intolerable series of atrocities. The conflict in Syria is intricate and complicated, as it involves multiple parties, preventing the Security Council from fulfilling its responsibilities and causing it to be a challenging issue for the UN to straighten things out. From the beginning, the UN has been engaged in upholding the protection of civilians affected by the ongoing conflict, together with humanitarian assistance, refugee support working with governments and other partners, diplomatic efforts like political negotiations, and human rights monitoring. But, all these are undermined if Syria is allowed to bomb hospitals and schools, use chemical weapons, torture civilians, withhold aid, and defy laws with an exemption from punishment.

Long back, we had hope. We inanely believed that we would be assured of international action if the people learned the truth about how we suffer. Today, we have the bitter question; "Why are we, the Syrian people, not worth saving?"

Aqeel paused his speech for a brief moment. Council members expressed their empathy by nodding in acknowledgement and maintaining a respectful silence. Riya's phone beeped with a message.

"I'm unfolding a map here, and this map helps to tell the story about the routes carved out of desperation into the European Union, particularly toward the more northern EU states that are often more likely to accept refugees."

Riya stepped out of her cabin and tried calling Wasim, but there was a network connection error. So, she sent him her location and entered the cabin again.

If you are not prepared to end the war, I wonder if you are mindful of your inescapable moral duty to help us to legal safety. Unless the war and conflicts come to an end, it is not safe or possible for refugees to return home. And no one knows when peace will return to our country. In the meantime, this refugee country has to be our home, and home should mean home. People reaching here have to be looked after with far more care and dignity.

The humanitarian actions taken for refugees are a make or break, but mostly a break. The grants for UNHCR have fallen far short of their actual, genuine demands. The UNHCR closed its books when only half of us were registered due to the failure of international politics and a lack of money. The situation is dire in the countries where we seek refuge. The count of refugees increases to millions, making up a significant portion of the entire population. This conveys that millions of refugees receive no support. Even the half of them registered are provided with a lesser amount of average monthly food expenditure, which is just what they need to survive.

For instance, in the camps of Bekaa Valley, Lebanon, people have been living in predominantly unstructured tents made of tarpaulin, plastic bags, cardboard and matchwood for years. It's the local NGOs making a magnificent effort to insulate tents and raise floors to prevent flooding. They have also established informal schools, about half in permanent buildings and half in tents. Around 65% of refugee children are now in some form of education. Still, most schools are left without any form of accreditation despite persistent efforts to appeal to international governments and education authorities for support.

It is possible to improve this situation with the big funders and their large partner organisations. As a matter of urgent priority, secure, workable financial platforms need to be regulated for transferring funds to our countries and the people to ensure that designated resources for aid and reconstruction reach their target. This would answer the question of political negligence and lack of care regarding international fund transfers for humanitarian work.

Besides this, there are other less evident vulnerabilities like tending to unaccompanied minors, the elderly, and others who are unable to care for themselves. Time and again, only the most obvious and visible challenges are identified during the clinical assessments. There is a general lack or limitation of access to primary health care, mental health care, treatment of chronic diseases, clinical management of rape, and legal abortion. There are women with high-risk pregnancies with limited access to proper follow-up and limited access to formula milk for newborn babies. The high number of unwanted pregnancies reveals the increased prevalence of SGBV (Sexual and Gender Based Violence). At this point, I appeal to the council to send signals that you are serious about holding the perpetrators accountable for sexual crimes."

Riya came out again and called Wasim.

"Wasim? Wasim, are you close?" asked Riya in a quavering voice as if she was about to cry the next second.

"What happened, Riya? Why do you sound like you are crying?"

"I don't know. I couldn't control it. I feel like crying. I do not know if this is your brother, but something inside me roars that he is Aqeel."

"But where did you see him? What's going on? I feel so lost, Riya. I have no idea what to ask you or what to do now. You asked me to come, and I'm already in the bus."

"Okay, okay. Let's calm down. Call me once you are here."

"Okay"

Riya waited for Wasim to disconnect the call. But as he didn't do it, she checked if he knew he was still on the line.

"Wasim? Still there?"

"Yes. Haven't you disconnected?"

Riya took a deep breath and said, "Come soon."

After a few seconds of silence, Wasim replied, "I love you," and cut the call.

"By now, the refugees had suffered a great deal. They faced a multitude of adversities, to which there is an added hindrance for those who are trying to rebuild their lives in their new surroundings and pursue their rights to seek security, health care, education, and employment.

Although Syrians have been proposed to offer temporary protection status, granting them access to services like schools and hospitals, they are often incapable of benefiting from the advantages. The registration system requires us to apply for work permits, but only 60,000 to 70,000 have been issued as of yet. Rejected applicants are given no reason for their rejection.

Most often, we are left to navigate the complicated asylum system on our own, with insufficient information and language support. The procedures are changed every year, and we cannot afford all the papers. We are forever anxious that we will be sent back. We leave our homeland, and we risk our lives. Don't you understand how desperate we need a safe place?"

Wasim had already reached and called Riya twice. As she didn't pick up the call, he waited for almost an hour, comprehending that she might not be in the situation to talk. He imagined and rehearsed what to speak to Aqeel, how Aqeel would respond, where to smile, and when to cry. He also tried hard to picture Aqeel, how he would look now, in the present. How much ever he tried, he could only see the little boy with curly hair and the pure, innocent smile.

Standing against the railings in front of the alley of flags, Wasim gazed at all the flags of various countries flying free in the air. He was trying to figure out where the flags of Syria and France were. At that moment, at the other end of the alley, he noticed Riya coming out with a young man from the entrance of the building. They walked straight along the exit road next to the alley. Wasim was stuck between watching them walk all the way down the road and turning his back on them in angst. He first turned away for a few seconds and held his chest in an effort to stop the heart from beating faster. He then turned towards them and watched the young man approaching him.

There was confidence in his walk, and he appeared perfectly poised. He was dressed impeccably in a well-tailored suit that accentuated his fit body frame and slightly tapered trousers, reaching just above his polished leather shoes. He was meticulously groomed, with neatly trimmed hair and a clean-shaven face displaying professionalism and sophistication.

While Wasim was still admiring, the young man came closer and stood right in front of him. Wasim had already forgotten everything that he had rehearsed. But the young man was in no need of words. He hugged Wasim so tightly as if he was trying to transfer all the love, he had missed giving in these ten years. Wasim was dumbfounded and yet not convinced that the young man was Aqeel, his brother.

He thought, "He looks like Aqeel, but he doesn't look like Aqeel. If this is Aqeel, thank goodness. But if this is not him, yet I accept him as my brother, my Aqeel will be left alone as an orphan. How do I make sure this is my brother? He believes that I'm his elder brother, and why couldn't I? Why am I sceptical?"

Releasing his grip slowly, the young man said, "Ya akhi, I understand that you are still unsure about who I am," and looked at Riya.

She smiled at him and moved next to Wasim to strengthen him.

The young man continued speaking, "It's fair that you don't recognize me. But I do. I do recognize this scar near your right eye." He gently touched it and stroked it, "I forced you to play frisbee in our backyard. While playing, I always threw it away from where you were standing. During one such throw, it flew near the new plant pots Ummi had bought a week ago. You ran to catch it and fell just on one of them, breaking the pot and getting hurt here," he pointed to the scar again.

Wasim, who couldn't handle his tears, hugged back at Aqeel. He cried out, letting his tears of joy run down his cheeks and kissing all over his brother's face. He hugged him again and lingered together just as though he didn't want to let him go again. Wasim saw Aqeel crying, too, so he wiped the tears away from his face, looking deeply into his eyes.

"Akhi, thank you for searching for me in all these years. I would have never seen you if you hadn't," said Aqeel.

"I have so much to talk to you and loads to ask from you. But for now, my mind and heart just want to delight in this joy. They couldn't think anything beyond that," said Wasim, holding Aqeel's hands.

"But I need to talk," said Riya on a serious note. They both looked at her, and she continued, "Let's go to my place and talk it all out."

# Chapter 15

On their way to Riya's apartment, Riya was consciously thinking about why was Aqeel's name involved in the mosque attack. How could someone eligible to give a speech in the UN be an accused? Of course, Aqeel is not guilty, but how could the truth be proved?

She looked at the brothers, to whom this complication never occurred, and they were chatting relentlessly, trying to pour out everything they had missed sharing for years.

At the apartment, when Aqeel went to get refreshed, Wasim and Riya had a quick conversation.

"I can see your face filled with relief," said Riya, sitting close to him.

"I could feel the immense weight lifted off my shoulders. I feel light. All thanks to you," said Wasim, getting close to her face. He rested his forehead on hers and closed his eyes, expressing peacefulness.

"Are you going to ask him about your parents now?" questioned Riya.

"Not now, of course. Maybe not today. I will ask about it tomorrow. If he is assuming that we three are together and I spill the beans that I've lost them too, he might also break into pieces. Let him sleep peacefully tonight, assured that I'm there for him now," replied Wasim.

"What if he knows something about them? Because your parents went in search of him, didn't they? If they were together..." doubted Riya.

"No, didn't you notice what he said? He thanked me for searching for him. He said if I hadn't, he would have been forever alone," said Wasim.

"No, he didn't say that," denied Riya.

Before Wasim could counter, Aqeel entered the room. Riya got up from the couch and gestured for Aqeel to sit beside his brother.

"I'll bring something to drink, what do you prefer?" asked Riya

"I'll have coffee, Riya. By the way, how should I address you?" asked Aqeel eagerly.

"Call me Riya, that's my name," said Riya and smiled.

"Yes, but... you are special to my brother. So, calling you Riya will not be appropriate," said Aqeel with a whimsical smile.

Riya beamed softly and went to her open kitchen, from where she could still see and talk with them both. Aqeel turned to his side to face Riya, who was making coffee and asked, "May I call you 'Ukhti'? I've never had a sister."

"Ukh... what?" stammered Riya.

"Ukh...ti, ukhti," helped Aqeel.

"Haaaannn, nice to hear. I like it," responded Riya as she enjoyed someone calling her sister.

She added, "So haven't I. I have never been called a sister, especially in Arabic," and laughed gracefully.

Riya was busy making coffee and taking a call from the office when the brothers resumed their conversation. After some time, she served them coffee and some refreshments.

"Aqeel, sorry to interrupt. But this is serious. Are you aware of what's happening to you right now?" asked Riya earnestly.

That was when Wasim brought the issue to his mind. He looked at Aqeel, terrified. Aqeel replied calmly,

"Are you asking about the mosque attack case?"

"Yes," nodded Riya.

"It's a huge hell of a story. But don't you both worry about it. I dealt with it already two days back," said Aqeel, looking at his brother with an assuring look.

"But, what was that? How did it all happen?" urged Riya.

"If I had been a little careful, we could have been together all these years. Do you remember that day, Akhi? I couldn't recollect what happened exactly. I just got a little lost from you, and in trying to find you, I must have gone farther away, it seems. There, I saw many people getting onto a bus and was carried away along with them. Expecting you three inside, I searched all through the bus and was let down. Crying, I went and stood near a woman who looked like our ummi. She called me and made me sit with her until we were disembarked. They transferred us to many different places and finally dumped us in the Zaatari camp in Jordan. There, I spent most of my time with an old woman and her grandson who…"

"I think they were who I met at the prefecture. Is the boy's name Adeel?" asked Riya eagerly.

"Yes," replied Aqeel, looking at her in surprise.

"They were the lead that helped reach you now," informed Riya.

"Did you meet them? Do you know where they are now? We had been together for many years," recalled Aqeel.

"I met them in France. I didn't get any of their contact numbers. But we can find them easily," said Riya.

"God is the best of the planners," exclaimed Aqeel and resumed his story,

*"I managed to survive there for nearly four years. And one day, many women and young children like me were taken to another camp near Iraq. Luckily, Adeel and his grandmother were among them accompanying me. But after three years, due to overcrowding, they took some of us to the Kilis refugee camp in Turkey, because of which we were separated. I didn't like it there. So, after a year of struggle, two other boys and I escaped from the camp and fell into another trap.*

*This particular camp, being near the Syrian border, we fell prey to the manipulation of one of the extremist groups in Syria. That was a time when we were vulnerable and grieving. They took advantage of it and promised us safety and a chance to fight for our cause. They also told us we belonged to Syria, offering us a sense of belonging and identity there. Desperate for a sense of belonging, we reluctantly agreed.*

*They promoted extremist ideas and educated us on different subjects and various issues. They made us feel powerful and used our frustration to their advantage. We were trained in weapon handling, basic medical aid, survival, and tactical skills. We were made to attend indoctrination sessions and be involved in ideological discussions. I was with them for around two years and excelled in everything in a very short period of time. I just enjoyed being there because they enabled me to fight against those who destroyed my home and separated me from my family. But I failed to be vigilant enough to discover their intentions were far from noble.*

*One day, I was approached by one of the heads of the group, and he asked me to execute an attack on a mosque in France. When I asked in detail, he showed me the picture of a person and incited me by saying that he was responsible for all our broken lives. He also explained to me how some innocent lives have to be sacrificed in the process of destroying an evil person. I accepted, even though I didn't feel it was right. Yet I started the journey to France reflecting on what am I going to do and for whom. My mind was filled with conflicting emotions and moral dilemmas. I couldn't shake off the unease that came with the idea of causing harm to innocent people, even if it was in pursuit of justice. On the way to Turkey, I met..."* Aqeel stopped talking.

"What happened?" asked Wasim.

Aqeel faced his brother as his face turned red, and he looked deep into his eyes.

"I met ummi and baba," said Aqeel.

Wasim swallowed his tears, trying to contain them. Those drops of tears burst out of his facial nerves. Finally, not being able to control them, he let them flow down silently.

"How are they?" Wasim asked in a tremulous voice.

"They are good, desolate, forlorn but still hoping to meet us again, together. Sometimes, against all odds, against all logic, and against all possibilities, we hope. We all hoped. And here we are getting together," replied Aqeel, briskly wiping off his tears.

Aqeel noticed Wasim resigning himself into deeper thoughts and didn't want to disturb him. So, he turned towards Riya to continue the story and end it as quickly as possible.

*"Meeting my parents after many years, I wanted to stay with them peacefully and didn't want to fight for any cause. So, I informed the organisation that I quit. But they were prudent by not aborting the plan; instead, they executed it with someone else and used my name. When I discussed this with my parents, they apprised me that Wasim would be in France. I decided to reach France intending to look for my brother and, at the same time, to stop the attack before the arrangements began.*

*I frequented that particular mosque twice before the attack to be sure of the location, which had now turned as evidence against me. Though regrettably, I couldn't impede the attack as they changed all the plans. In those few months in France, life gave me better things to do. I got to meet many people from an NGO called Hand in Hand for Syria who witnessed the elocution skill in me that I developed while I was with the extremist group. Today, I turned out to be a representative to speak on behalf of the Syrian refugees in the UN."*

"Those tiny little feet and hands are now doing great things. You have grown up a lot," uttered Wasim, looking at his brother affectionately.

* * *

After talking about lots and lots of stuff, finally, the three went to sleep. Riya slept, confidently convinced that Wasim would sleep peacefully that night. But he got out of bed after confirming that Riya was asleep and came to the balcony. Aqeel, who was already standing out on the balcony, offered his brother a seat, and he sat on another chair.

"Didn't sleep yet?" asked Aqeel.

"I miss them very much," Wasim whispered sadly.

"Inviting them here is infeasible due to several factors like refugee status, visa requirements, application process, and consular discretion. It would be better if we go there," insisted Aqeel.

"To where?" questioned Wasim edgily.

"To Turkey. That's where they are. The same house we stayed in then. Baba said he doesn't want us to search for them all over Turkey. So, they both decided to live in the same house so we could find them easily," said Aqeel and stopped.

Turning towards Wasim, he asked, "Akhi, shall we leave for Turkey?"

"Yes, yes. We should," said Wasim thoughtfully with a fixed gaze.

"What are you thinking about?" asked Aqeel.

"Nothing, I'll do the ticket arrangements," said Wasim, taking his phone out of his pocket.

"But, I don't have papers. I came here illegally," said Aqeel, looking at his brother and thinking about how he was going to react.

Wasim stood up, walked near the railing and held it tight. He recollected all the pain he endured from Syria to France in the course of building a new life in a new country. He could imagine how his brother would have suffered too. But he didn't want to bring that up. So, he quickly reacted,

"We shall go by car. We will start tomorrow. Get everything set," said Wasim and went inside as Aqeel followed him. They both went to their beds but couldn't sleep.

* * *

The next day, Riya woke them up with wake-up coffee. But to her surprise, Aqeel wanted to get refreshed before coffee, just like Wasim. She smiled at their alikeness and waited for them both to join her.

"Riya, I want to meet my parents immediately. But the problem is Aqeel is here without papers. So, I decided to drive down to Turkey. Today. Would you be able to come along?" briefed Wasim and desired Riya to accompany him.

"But why drive? How about a train?" suggested Riya.

"It's riskier. Aqeel may get his papers checked. Travelling by road is less risky," said Wasim.

"Ok. I have some important affairs to handle tomorrow. You guys start. I will take the flight from here and join you in Sofia. Does that work for you?" asked Riya while Aqeel joined the discussion.

"Of course, yes," agreed Aqeel.

* * *

Before Riya left for her office, Wasim and Aqeel started.

The same route that Wasim dreaded for years, the route that Wasim never wanted to go back to, has now allured him. From Geneva, a small diversion into France, then Italy, Slovenia, Croatia, Serbia, and Bulgaria. He was stuck between hell and the anticipated happiness. Remembrances of the hideous past and the imagination of his envisioned joy were feuding inside him.

But this time, he didn't share them with his brother. Instead, he was a listener hearing out his brother's story. They drove and drove until Wasim grew tired.

"Once you come to France with all the papers, learn to drive. I can't manage it alone," said Wasim contentedly.

"Let's stop and take a break. You get some sleep before we resume," said Aqeel, and they stopped near Padua, Italy.

Wasim reclined his seat and laid back to relax when Aqeel got out of the car and called his parents to inform them that he had seen Wasim and they were on the way to Turkey. He also gave them a heads-up about Riya so they don't react unfavourably. After an hour of rest and a coffee, the journey continued.

They reached Sofia Airport in twenty-eight hours with a few short breaks and a night's stay inside the car. Riya, who arrived at the airport, joined them and drove the car to give Wasim some rest.

"Aqeel, travelling within the EU countries is no big deal. Now, getting into Turkey might raise concerns and pose a problem. I spoke with an immigration lawyer, and he suggested not to enter Turkey as it could result in deportation," advised Riya.

"What do we do now?" asked Wasim anxiously.

"Let's not enter Turkey. We will meet them at the border," said Riya, looking at Wasim. He was blank. She then looked at Aqeel through the rearview mirror.

Aqeel looked back at Riya with a confident look on his face and said, "Edirne. The place that parted us is going to witness the union."

Listening to what he said, Wasim's heart brimmed with happiness. His lips moved to smile, but he brought them under control. However, his contended eyes didn't fail to show the amount of joy he was experiencing.

After nearly three hours of driving, they sighted a few cars parked on both sides of the road. Google Maps notified, 'Your destination is on your right.' For every inch they moved on the road, Wasim's heart pounded faster and, at the same time, rejoiced to see his parents. He stopped talking and remained silent.

A few metres before the gate at Pazarkule Border Crossing Point in Edirne, they pulled off the road and asked Aqeel to check if they had come. Aqeel called their parents. After talking to them, he informed Wasim and Riya that they would reach in another twenty minutes. Wasim couldn't sit idly inside the car, so he got out of the car and wandered up and down.

It had been thirty minutes, and Wasim struggled to keep his excitement in check. He started walking towards the gate. Noticing him, Riya and Aqeel got out of the car and ran behind Wasim, who sat on a bench just in front of the gate. Aqeel accompanied him on the bench without speaking a word. Riya put her hand on Wasim's shoulder to comfort him. Wasim, when he lifted his head to look at Riya, saw an old couple standing far away on the other side of the gate.

Before he could realise it was his parents and run towards them, the sky opened up, and it poured out of nowhere, followed by a blaring thunder. The rain came down in a flash as if a veiled reservoir had been let out unbound. The strong breeze was quickly filled with the lovely scent of rain-soaked earth. The raindrops pattering on the rooftops and cars filled the atmosphere with an intense sound. The suddenness of the rain drove all the people and creatures alike to seek shelter. All the border control police rushed into their tents and booths as if they had abandoned the entire place for Wasim's family. It was as if nature had chosen this moment to remind them of its power and ability.

As Wasim started running forward, his surroundings blurred, and his focus narrowed to his parents. At that point in time, he forgot all the miseries that had happened to them. The only thing in his mind was to start living from where he stopped. He wanted to be cared for and nursed by them, which he had missed in all these years. He wanted to lie down on his father's lap and his mother to caress his forehead. He wanted to eat his favourite Syrian kibbeh cooked by his mother. He wanted to have his father beside him and listen to all that he said.

Wasim couldn't restrain his body from falling on his mother and father and clung to them. He held them tight with both hands and panted to catch his breath. Being able to hold her treasure that she had thought was lost gave a novel feeling to his mother. Not just butterflies, but she had a whole lot of a zoo in her stomach. She fell on her knees and cried out in ecstasy. His father locked his eyes on Wasim, and for a moment, he could neither move nor breathe. His lips trembled as he whispered Wasim's name under his breath. He enveloped him in a tight, tearful embrace and felt like he had regained his biggest strength. He brushed Wasim's hair at the back, trying to study and etch every detail of him into his memory. An avalanche of emotions surged through everyone's hearts, taking no notice of the rain. No border control officials came forward to interfere and keep them within bounds. In truth, they silently appreciated the reunion as they were dissatisfied with doing a brutal job every day.

By this time, Aqeel had joined the three and hugged them together. Then, as the reality of the reunion sank in, a rush of emotions burst forth. And as both the rain and the emotions subsided, they sat down together. They laughed through tears—a laugh filled with astonishment and amazement.

They talked about their past, present, and future. They talked about their home. They talked about starting the reunification process. They talked about Wasim and Riya.

155